Running on Full

Tina Sharma Tiwari

Rupa & Co

The author asserts the moral right to be identified
as the author of this work.

Typeset by
Mindways Design
1410 Chiranjiv Tower
43 Nehru Place
New Delhi 110 019

Printed in India by
Shree Maitrey Printech Pvt Ltd.
A-84, Sector-2, Noida

To Manishi,
for putting up with me

Contents

Acknowledgements

There are so many people who are responsible in ways big and small, for this book being a reality today. I thank every single person who has crossed my path, even if briefly, for either inspiring me or infuriating me or loving me or hating me. All these experiences, places and people have fuelled my imagination for this narrative, but I would like to stress here that this is a work of fiction.

There are some people in particular, without whose support this book would not have been possible, and I acknowledge them here.

My sister Tarang, for being my one-woman cheerleading squad for over three decades.

My mother, for cracking the whip and leaving no scope for incompetence, ever.

My father, for being the balm.

Chandru, for being my sounding-board for this manuscript and everything else.

Vivian Loke, for showing me, a million years ago, how much fun life can be.

Priya Gopalan, for being subjected to the first draft of this manuscript and surviving it.

My publishers, Rupa & Co. for believing in a first-time author.

My editor Ankush, whose sardonic critiques helped make the manuscript what it is today.

Rashmi, on Rupa's editorial team for helping me stay positive.

My first love, for starting a new chapter in my life.

My lost love, for making me believe impossible is nothing.

And most of all, my lasting love for being my pillar, my friend, my partner and my angel.

One

Prudential Is Not the Word

It was about three in the afternoon and the sun was fierce. The dust danced on the road every time a vehicle trundled past, settling down sluggishly as if also sapped from the heat. My mother, sister and I stood, wilting, at the bus stop on the main road that ran perpendicular to the lane of our colony. I absently drew patterns in the dirt with my open-toed sandals, unaware that the day unfolding before us would change the history of the nation.

'Villagers!' mother snapped as a man spat out a stream of betel juice barely a metre away from us. The man glowered back in her direction, but she had already turned to the opposite direction, her red chiffon sari fluttering in the wind.

I was six years old and we lived in what was apparently an overgrown village, according to my mother – a woman of elegance that far belied her modest upbringing. At a young age she had earned herself a scholarship to a prestigious boarding school for little princesses and fancied herself no less than royalty. She would talk of privy purses being abolished by Prime Minister Indira Gandhi as though it had something to do with us standing at a bus stop in a dreary suburb of the capital, waiting for a rickety, overloaded bus.

To me however, our environment didn't seem in the least bit rural. My father owned a scooter not a bullock-cart, and our roads were paved. But apartments were still unheard of, electricity and water supplies played fickle games and dusty by-lanes were a reality we lived and played in everyday.

'Why are there so few people on the roads?' I asked, looking up at her after taking in the meagre crowd around us. Normally on a Saturday, when we went to our grandfather's home, we would have to wrestle and kick to find a seat on the bus. But this felt like a Sunday evening when Doordarshan would telecast a feature film and the streets would be eerily deserted. Satellite television was ten years ahead in our future, and DVD technology would not reach India until two decades later.

'They're all listening to and watching some stupid match,' my mother answered, peering through her oversized sunglasses at the empty road with no sign of a bus.

'What match?' Shiny and I asked together. Match meant cricket, we knew that much. But we had never known a cricket match to parallel the Sunday movie in its ability to keep people indoors.

'Oh, I don't know. They call it the World Cup or something,' she said with a hint of irritation. 'Even your father must be watching it in his office.'

'Is that why he's gone to office?' I asked, suddenly suspicious. It was unusual for my father to be at work on Saturday, and they did have a television set there. What was the big deal about this match anyway? I turned my attention to an ugly, snotty baby draped over his mother's shoulder, wearing a woollen cap in the June heat and a big black dot on his forehead.

'What are we going to eat at Gashaji's?' I said, wondering aloud.

Our little nuclear unit of four lived in a suburban government colony, miles away from the city centre. Over the weekends I remember being in my maternal grandfather, Gashaji's bungalow in South Delhi. My father was a government officer, but unfortunately an honest one – tons of respect but no money. And as my mother explained to us when we were older, it was easier to make ends meet with two people working instead of four. Whatever the reasons, Shiny and I were blissfully unaware and eternally delighted to be deposited at Gashaji's. Like the ideal grandfather, he allowed us to watch movies round the clock, and wolf on ice cream and chips until we were ready to be sick. Moreover, he would lie to our mother every time she arrived to pick us up on Sunday evening: 'Of course they've done their homework. No, I haven't let them watch any videos,' he would say, winking at us all the while.

No wonder then, our cousins Kartik and Saurav were also almost always there. They were my father's elder brother's sons and lived a block away from Gashaji. So every time they heard that Shiny and me were around, they came over to join the party. We would make Kartik and Saurav play girlie games like hopscotch on the terrace, and they would try to convince us to wrestle. While I would gladly oblige, Shiny wouldn't. I would also almost always beat both boys – all it required of me was to try and sit on them as I was nearly double their weight. But Kartik would still insist every time. He was like that. Kartik would also dare me to jump from the terrace down to the lawns, and I did it to prove I was just as brave. I never broke a bone, but he did. Twice.

So that was life back then. A little bit of school, a whole lot of fun: curly-haired Kartik with his perpetual knee scabs, mild-mannered Saurav sporting his eternal grin, saintly Shiny with her buckteeth and fountain ponytail, and me, porky the pig. But everything would change during the summer. Summer holidays were when the rest of the Trivedi kin from all over the country would assemble in Delhi and life would suddenly become very exciting. My father's eldest and youngest brothers lived in Mumbai. To us, it seemed a different planet. '*Moochh Tauji*' was a pilot in Air India and his bushy moustache was much like the mascot maharaja's. Their little third-floor apartment in Juhu was full of the most magnificent things from all over the world. There was a cuckoo clock from Germany, which I would observe for hours, anticipating the cuckoo any moment. There was a huge colour-television and countless videotapes of Disney cartoons. They even had a remarkable brown car named Mercedes. It was a little overwhelming and the Delhi quartet was perpetually in awe of his kids, Meetu *Didda* and Ratan.

'Will Kartik and Saurav be there too?' Shiny asked, hopeful. We were finally seated on a bus and the only way to survive the mind-numbing one-and-a-half-hour journey ahead was to chatter all the way.

'Yes, I think so. Even Meetu and Ratan might be there,' mother answered. I shuddered with excitement at the thought of a houseful of cousins.

'What fun!' I exclaimed, jumping up and down on my seat for effect.

'Don't get too excited,' I was warned. 'Gashaji has a colour TV, remember? I'm sure everyone would be busy watching cricket. Maybe you can play with Meetu for a change.'

What she meant was the boys would be preoccupied. She was never too comfortable with our roughhousing, and made no bones about the fact that she would prefer us to play with girls, just like girls were supposed to. Watching us climb trees and drainpipes with Kartik and Saurav gave her ulcers. She was more favourable towards the Mumbai cousins.

Meetu *Didda* and Ratan were always a little different. *Didda* was not just older by five years, but also very aware of her 'cool' status. Stylish, pretty and hip, she listened to Madonna on her personal portable stereo, and told us what London and New York were like. Needless to say, I was full of admiration for her. But Ratan, elder to me by two years, was something else. He hadn't acquired a shred of the sophistication that comes with being well-travelled and moneyed. Pale, skinny and sickly, he wouldn't ever sleep over at anyone else's place because he missed his Mommy too much. Even at the age of six, Kartik and I knew that was not cool. He would read comics of strange creatures like Bananaman and Mighty Mouse, the latter eventually leading to the apt nickname of Ratman. And every time Kartik or I would suggest a wrestling match, Ratan would politely decline and not even offer a reason! What a bizarre boy he was.

Shiny had to be shaken awake when we finally arrived at Hauz Khas at close to five in the evening, sweaty and dusty from the ride. It was a short walk from the bus stop to my grandfather's but our legs felt heavy like lead and Mummy had to actually carry Shiny. There wasn't a soul in sight.

'Is the match still going on?' I inquired. I had never felt inclined to watch a single minute of cricket in my life, let alone an entire match. So many skinny men dressed in white pants walking around and scratching their crotches as if they needed to pee. It seemed simply too boring to me. Papa had taken me along to the football stadium during the '82 Asian Games the year before, and that had been an exhilarating experience. Although I hadn't followed much of the proceedings, the riot of colour, the chants of the crowd and my resplendent golden satin jacket had made the atmosphere electric. I remembered it was over in a flash. Didn't matches last just a couple of hours? In our colony, when the boys played cricket it lasted about half an hour at most. So what was this about?

'Cricket matches last for days. Five days,' mother informed us. 'And then too, they end in a draw.'

'Then what's the point?' I giggled, sucking up to my mother by echoing her unmistakable contempt for cricket. Ignoring my question she continued, 'But this one's different, this Prudential Cup thing. This time they are playing only one-day matches.'

'The whole day?' Shiny asked wide-eyed, perched in my mother's arms and looking into her face from an inch away. 'Don't they get tired?'

'No, it's not like tennis or swimming,' mother said. 'They don't even run. They just stand around and tap the ball with the bat.'

As we came to the white iron gate, the portly figure of Gashaji appeared from the living room veranda, radiant in his distinctive combination of *kurta-pyjama* and beret.

'Aajao, aajao!' he bellowed as Shiny and I threw ourselves into his arms, squeezed his podgy shoulders and took in the unmistakable scent of Old Spice. The entire troupe walked in behind him – Kartik, Saurav, *Didda*, Ratan and even our youngest uncle Neel *Chacha*! He was the unanimous favourite, always full of jokes and improbable tales.

I greeted the gang cheerily, immediately announcing that we should all run up to the terrace to play Chor-Police, the Hindi film-inspired version of cops and robbers. But there were no takers for my suggestion. All the boys mumbled something about the match and darted off indoors. I couldn't believe it – Kartik had practically ignored me. Not that they had ever disliked each other, but Kartik and Ratan were getting along particularly well this time round and the equations were changing somehow. And Ratan had also adopted a new fad – that of hating girls. At first I didn't take particular umbrage to it, until Ratan pointedly mentioned that I belonged under that category and therefore would be excused from the sacred cricket ceremony taking place inside the living room.

It hit me hard. Until then, the girl had always been Shiny. She was the one who played with dolls, was afraid of bees and didn't wrestle. As for me, I was no different from Kartik or Saurav. In fact I did a much better job of being a boy than that stupid Ratan himself. I was absolutely furious but couldn't understand why. All fortnight, since the Mumbai Cousins had descended upon Delhi, Ratan had been behaving like that. Kartik and him had been bonding over some people called Kapil and Kirti and Kris. It suddenly dawned upon me that he was trying to steal Kartik away from me, using cricket as the bait! He was paying me back for all those years of bullying and being very smart about it.

'I hate cricket!' I yelled at no one in particular. 'I HATE IT! I HATE IT!'

But the boys paid me absolutely no attention and neither did any of the grown-ups who were around. I had no choice but to swallow my pride and follow everyone into the house, in front of the telly.

'India is batting first,' Kartik told me as if it were supposed to make some sense to me. Everyone around the room nodded gravely for some reason. Neel *Chacha* continued, 'We're going to be all out for less than 200.'

What on Earth was everybody talking about? All through the evening Ratan maintained his efforts to irritate me. He would quietly say something insulting about fat girls and then look decidedly in my direction. I would take the bait, erupt and charge at him like a mad bull. No one had dared call me fat on my face before. Of course, I knew I was a bit chubby but had never cared. Suddenly I had visions of growing up tall, slim, beautiful and even blonde, like Darryl Hannah in Splash. That would serve Ratan right. But meanwhile, he was relentless even though he got beaten up quite a few times in the process. He had found my touchy nerve.

As the evening progressed, more and more people from the neighborhood filtered into the lone house with the colour television. Papa also walked in at some point, as did the remainder of his clan. Mummy got busy preparing a Kashmiri feast for everyone and the odours emanating from the kitchen soon had my stomach rumbling. Why wasn't anyone else interested in eating just yet?

I had gathered by now that India were pitted against some team called West Indies with tall, black men. There was even something decidedly exciting about the way some of them ran in towards the batsman, a menacing glare in their eyes, but I was not about to admit that I was actually enjoying something in that dull, grainy telecast. The mood in the room oscillated wildly between elation to gloom and then, bewildering me, back to joy. Somewhere in the middle of the match the television went blank. Groans and curses were uttered all around. Doordarshan had apparently lost the signal. I found my cue.

'Let's all go and play outside,' I said, looking around hopefully at all my cousins. 'How about hide-n-seek?'

Shiny and *Didda* were more than happy to jump off the sofa, but the boys still seemed reluctant. I couldn't fathom why. Somebody said the match was lost anyway, leading to animated disagreement from everyone else. Somebody else shouted out for the radio to be turned on. Just as the women folk started re-emerging from the shadows and people started talking about saner things like food, the darn match came back on.

After that, the world around me went nuts. Gashaji's bungalow turned into a madhouse. Every few minutes there would be a collective roar of 'Out!' as though someone was being banished from a kingdom. I had never seen the adults in my family act like lunatics before. It was very disconcerting. Names like Jimmy, Kapil and Gavaskar were being chanted like a prayer. And then suddenly, like the bursting of a balloon full of confetti, India won. And everybody went absolutely bananas. Papa lifted Neel *Chacha* off the ground in joy, Kartik, Ratan, and even Saurav jumped on the sofa, knocking a bowl of chips over, Gashaji hugged Kartik's father, and all the ladies clapped wildly. I tried to join in the hullabaloo but couldn't find the inspiration. India may have won this World Cup thing but I had lost my best friend.

Later that night, amidst crackers and crazed dancing on the streets, we staged one of our family races. Family races were held when all of us had to go somewhere in multiple cars. Then, Papa and his brothers would get behind the wheels, the children would takes sides and everyone would screech to the destination. Rajesh *Tauji*, Kartik's father, was the best bet. Not only because he was usually the fastest, but also because he was the only one who had no qualms whatsoever disobeying traffic signals and thereby thrilling us to the core.

All of us were scrambling to get into Rajesh *Tauji's* Fiat. I raced to what traditionally was mine – the front seat. Ratan was already sitting there, smug little pasty-white face, but there was room for one more. Just as I was about to slide in next to him holding aloft my third ice lolly, Ratan placed his hand on the seat and said, 'Reserved.'

I stared at him, dumbstruck. 'What do you mean reserved?' I managed to say, the Mango Duet dripping on my fingers.

'The front seat is not for girls,' he said, like some high and mighty lord. I couldn't believe what I had just heard. I itched to say something highly rude and insulting, but all that escaped me was, 'Huh?'

Meanwhile, Kartik came rushing in, past me, and jumped into the seat just as Ratan deftly removed his hand.

'I'm Kapil!' 'I'm Jimmy!' they hollered at each other in delight.

'Kartik?' I asked, incredulous. Kartik shifted somewhat uncomfortably and just shrugged. He wouldn't look me in the eye. My heart broke instantly. Sadly, I turned to the back seat and to my horror it was full. Shiny and Saurav were chatting away happily and Suchitra Tai had taken her rightful place in her husband's car. *Didda* called out to me from some other car and I trudged towards it, so dejected that I wanted to toss the ice cream bar.

Everything after that was a blur. I never even noticed who won the inane race, because my whole existence had just changed. Life, as I knew it, was over. It was no longer Kartik and me, best friends and bullies of the world.

I decided I would never speak to Ratan again. And I would wish the game of cricket into oblivion.

Two

Quite So Logically

It was Mumbai in the mid-1980s and a government colony in Wadala was the most important place in the universe. Not least because it housed me, the eight-year-old master of that universe. My father had been transferred to the business capital of the country and Shiny and I took to the new life like fish to water.

The colony was Hans Christen Andersen's dream – it was absolutely infested with little people. Yes, there were some adults too, but they were so grossly outnumbered and inconsequential, that I can hardly remember any. In any case they were happy to blend in with the background and leave the governance to us.

And we ran it with aplomb. When construction labourers descended upon the colony to convert the beloved badminton court into a pump house, we diligently formed 'Shivaji's Army' and drove them away with sticks and stones. When the pumphouse was eventually built – even the valiant fight some losing battles

– we busted a smuggling racket in it. Sadly though, the smugglers got away. We converted a banana grove into a most elegant secret chamber with stools, rugs and even teacups pilfered from our various homes.

There was the girls' gang and the boys' gang. Thanks to my girl-hating cousin Ratan and my mother's open despondency at not having had a son, I had a huge chip on my shoulder. Secretly ashamed, openly defiant. I led the girls' gang with a dedication so fierce that I managed to fool everyone. The leader of the boy's bunch was Bunty *Bhaiyya* – a gangly boy with a grin so wide it looked it had been pinned from ear to ear. The *'bhaiyya'* tag was ubiquitous because he was a good five years older than most of us, a ripe old thirteen.

Despite being so old, he still liked to play in the evenings. All the girls his age, the *'didis'*, would only come out for walks. They would all walk in a tight cluster, take endless rounds of the colony and giggle as if something were perpetually funny. We didn't think very much of them. The *bhaiyyas* were a more comprehensible species. They would come out to play quite often, but not always. Sometimes they complained about studies as if it were some kind of illness. 'No I can't come out today because I have to study.' The excuse didn't hold much weight with us because we would have homework too. But perhaps not everyone was as bright, so we let them be.

Bunty was different, as he never wanted to study. So, much to the delight of the boys' gang, this big gangly *bhaiyya* was always available to beat the girls at dodge ball, seven stones –you name it. We gave a good fight though.

Every evening, the ritual was the same. Shiny and I would return from school and before we could race out to freedom, a tall glass of milk stood in our way. I treated the obstacle like a dose of medicine – down in a shot and forgotten till tomorrow. But poor Shiny would agonise over it, taking little sips and gagging on each one. I never had the patience to wait for her so I would run out and get the rest of the battalion ready. The battleground was always the open space directly behind my house. We didn't have much of a choice, as it was the only space in the colony big enough to pass for a playground, other than the badminton court. This was Mumbai; space was at a premium. So the boys' and girls' teams would assemble, two four-feet-tall walls facing each other across the dusty playground. The game of the day would then be decided, usually after a quick conference between Bunty, me and a few of our trusted aides. And then all hell would break loose. Had an outsider chanced upon our colony during one of the girls-versus-boys games, they would have thought a generation of barbarians was being bred.

'Kill them!'

'Finish him off!'

During one such contest that summer, tempers rose a few degrees higher than usual. Someone said, 'Boys are so stupid.' A collective roar was followed by the smartest, most insulting line any of us had ever heard.

'Girls are not nice, because their hair is full of lice,' Bunty said with a smugness that revealed days of rehearsal. I was instantly furious.

'How dare you? All of us don't have lice!' I said indignantly, but somehow that didn't have the same stinging effect as Bunty's rhyming one-liner.

All the boys chorused, 'You do! You do!' And lots of boos.

I had to do something. Quick.

Well, there was always one sure-shot solution to any problem: Papa. It was a Sunday and he was home. Without any sort of explanation I darted round the corner and disappeared into my house. I went screaming and wailing into the living room, where Papa was having a cup of tea in front of the gleaming new black-and-white television set. He was watching a very light-haired boy who looked like an albino playing tennis. Not allowing myself to get distracted, I told Papa about our humiliation and the urgency of the situation. I begged him to come up with a smarter retort, and fast. My father surprised even me with his wisdom and lightning speed.

Immediately he said, 'Boys are very naughty and they're even worse than potty.'

Ho! I couldn't believe how good it was. Papa had just reinforced the fact that he was simply the best. As my mother entered the room, a silver tray of biscuits nestled in hand, I grabbed two and raced back out, repeating the rhyme under my breath lest I forget it, thrilled at the prospect of barking it at Bunty. Meanwhile, Molly, my second-in-command, had scrambled in after me to see why their leader had suddenly deserted them like a coward. Her eyes sparkled when I told her, making her look even more doll-like than usual; with her silken straight hair, dainty nose and rosebud lips, Molly was living proof that it was possible to be a stunner even at seven.

We both returned to the playground, and first created an atmosphere of mystery. Everybody just stared at us expectantly. Then Molly and I whispered it to Shiny, Molly's younger sister Polly, and a few other girls around us. We suppressed giggles even as the boys looked more and more confused. Then with an air of finality, I crossed my arms and gave the signal for a collective chorus.

'BOYS ARE VERY NAUGHTY AND THEY'RE EVEN WORSE THAN POTTY!'

They were beaten, shocked. All fifteen or so looked like the wind had been sucked out of them. They couldn't possibly come up with something better than that. So I decided to add insult to injury and said, 'And a boy told us that.'

There were groans of disbelief.

'That's not even possible,' Bunty said. 'None of us said that.'

'It's true!' Molly said, adding to the intrigue.

A massive argument ensued, during the course of which it was divulged that my father was the remarkable poet in question. Without a warning, all the boys charged into my house and we girls trooped in behind them. My father was still in the living room, trying to finish that cup of tea and watch the match in peace. He wasn't allowed to.

'Uncle it's not fair! How can you make a poem against boys?' Bunty demanded, on the verge of tears. The rest of the boys made some more indistinguishable noises. The fact that my father only laughed was not lost on any of us – girls or boys – as a very peculiar reaction.

There was so much disagreement in the air that nobody wanted to play anymore. Either way, it was growing dark outside and we would have been called in sooner or later. As everyone left, Shiny and I joined our parents, attacked the divine chocolate-cream biscuits and tried to comprehend the flickering images before us.

'Who's that?' I asked about the strawberry-blond boy who was now swinging his racket down as though swatting a fly that had irked him beyond forgiveness.

'His name is Boris Becker,' Mummy answered. 'He's only seventeen years old.'

Only seventeen? Seventeen sounded quite old to me.

'Is he going to win?' Shiny asked my parents, the fountain ponytail on top of her head bobbing as she spoke animatedly. We both knew this was something called Wimbledon, and to win here was considered very prestigious in tennis. My mother being far more favourable towards tennis than cricket had educated us on the basics. But we had never seen a tennis court in life, let alone try our hand at the sport.

'Papa, do you know how to play tennis?' I asked, aware that my father had been an avid sportsman in his college years.

'Not really,' he replied. 'I tried playing once or twice. I was more of a squash player.'

Squash. The only squash I knew was orange squash and that was drunk, not played. I shrugged and tried to make sense of what was happening.

'He's West German,' Mummy said to Papa, who nodded. 'Has there been a German champion before?'

'I don't think so,' Papa replied. 'And he's unseeded.'

'What does that mean, unseeded?' Shiny and I asked together. It was a very interesting word. As if tennis champions were grown on a farm and this one had sprouted by chance.

'It means he doesn't have a ranking; he's a nobody,' announced Mummy, confusing us even more. Later I would grow up to realise that the explanation wasn't just vague, it was also entirely wrong. A seeding is like a temporary ranking awarded by the tournament, largely dependent on the player's world rating but also on how much of a chance the tournament directors think that player has of winning that particular event. You could be world number one but seeded two at a particular grand slam.

But back then, that was all the explanation we got, as we were riveted by the images of this miraculous 'unseeded' teenager dancing on court like a lunatic, flinging himself around and pumping his fists like an animal. I had never witnessed emotion like that — raw, powerful and unleashed. It was a magical moment, and I was spellbound for life.

As the seventeen-year-old fellow raised the silver trophy above his head I mentally made notes for what I would describe the next day to all my friends. After all, there was a birthday party to attend and I would have a ready audience.

Birthday parties in the colony were great. There were fancy-dress competitions, singing contests and games like passing-the-parcel, not to mention the food — club sandwiches, *choley bhature*, gooey cake and ice cream. Birthdays were also the big social dos when all the unimportant people of the colony would suddenly become significant because they gave money for the gifts. But they still weren't invited. That would have been social sacrilege. No, birthdays were exclusively for us, to turn out in our finery and compete for as many prizes as possible.

That year Chintu threw a really big bash. Other than the completion of his sixth year, Chintu was celebrating another feat. From then on he was going to be known as Kapil, and he had chosen the name himself. To us that was inconceivable, but upon questioning, his parents confirmed it to be true.

'Are you going to change your name at school as well?' we asked the boy who was now Kapil.

'Of course,' he shrugged. 'It's already been done.'

We were all so impressed, especially Shiny. She had nursed a crush on him ever since the two had stepped out of their diapers.

'Why Kapil?' I asked him, mouth full of noodles.

'Because I want to be Kapil Dev,' he answered matter-of-factly. By now I knew that Kapil Dev was the biggest cricket icon in

India. He was God to any boy who was not old enough to know he wasn't going to grow up to be a professional cricketer.

I accepted the rather extraordinary answer, still marvelling at the fact that he had been allowed to christen himself. Just as I began to ponder if I would be allowed to rename myself Boris, Sanjana walked in. None of us liked her because she recycled birthday gifts. She handed the birthday boy one of those dubious packages and then herself said 'Thank you', even before he could.

We thought it was outrageous and Molly, Polly, Shiny and I cracked up instantly. Saying 'thank you' after giving the gift, what was she thinking? Bunty *bhaiyya* came to Sanjana's rescue, though we couldn't understand why. All four of us were exceedingly irritated when he cut short our guffaws, telling her, 'It's okay.' He was our friend, not hers.

'What do you mean it's okay?' I demanded. 'Chintu is supposed to say thank you, not her!' And that's when it came.

'Logically,' he said, 'it makes sense. She's thanking him for accepting it.'

Lojickly? What was that? That was an alien word, it didn't mean anything. What language was Bunty speaking?

'What's lojickly?' the four of us chimed in with confused amusement. We thought the word had a most quizzical, comical sound to it.

'How do I explain logically?' Bunty asked no one in particular. And that set us off again. We choked with giggles, repeating the word 'lojickly' over and over, delighting in the sound it produced.

'Mister Lojickly' Polly, the undisputed joker in our quartet, suddenly said to Bunty. Oh how quick-witted we thought that was! Immediately the rest of us caught on, and the room was echoing with yells of 'Mr Lojickly' and giggles. An exasperated Bunty walked off to join another group while I refocused my attention on the divine pineapple cake. But the Mr Lojickly business was far from over.

From then on, it was always 'Mr Lojickly'. Whenever Bunty stepped out of his house, someone would yell, 'Mr Lojickly' from a balcony somewhere. If he did something stupid on the playing field, 'Mr Lojickly' was the one taunted. Every time Bunty tried to intimidate the girls' gang, we had our eternal trump card. You get the drift.

That Diwali, all the *bhaiyyas* were putting up a special fireworks display for the whole colony, on top of the water tanks. It was quite spectacular but the girls were preoccupied with a secret plan. We were going to publicly humiliate the leader of the opposition.

Just as the rockets went off, uncles and aunties began to clap and the big boys started celebrating on the pump-house roof, the girls started a chant of their own.

'Yes, actually, Mr Logically. Yes, actually, Mr Logically,' over and over, and louder than the Diwali bombs.

We thought it was a brilliant and incisive insult. We all went home late that night, thrilled with ourselves.

Nothing really changed though, until one evening when a bicycle race was the decided competition of the day. Somebody had got himself or herself a new machine, and cycle fever had infected everyone. Those of us who didn't own cycles – Shiny and me included – could rent one from Jagdish's shop across the road, for one rupee and no time limit. You just had to return it the same day, that was all. So some of us were on rented bikes and some on purchased ones, but the entire sub-14 population of the colony was pedalling furiously that day. I would love to have given Bunty a run for his money, but he was more than a lap ahead of me and decided to rub it in. All of a sudden he came up from behind and thwacked me on the head. I was so startled that I lost control of my bike, which was anyway too big for me. I had pompously asked Jagdish to give me an adult-sized men's cycle as it was a symbol of bravery to ride one of those. I came crashing down, arms and legs flailing in all directions. A few metres ahead, Bunty skidded to a halt and looked apologetic. But upon seeing my wrath, he decided to make a run for it. A few spectators had collected meanwhile. I decided I was going to get my revenge.

I struggled out from under the tangled metal, threw the bike off to one side and picked up a large twig. To finish the race Bunty had to come back this way at least twice. And I was waiting in position, armed with the twig and ready to smack his head off. But when he did arrive, I decided that going for his bike was a more legally acceptable option.

'Go Die!' I screamed and lashed out at the tyre.

Bunty easily swerved and I missed. A few metres ahead, he turned around with the oddest expression on his face and said, 'I'm already dead . . . dead in love with you,' and quickly sped off. I didn't see him again the rest of that evening.

I was too stunned, not because I understood what that meant, but because I didn't.

'Huh? What does that mean?' I asked everyone in general and no one in particular.

'That means he likes you,' offered Tinkle *didi*, Chintu's elder sister who had magically appeared upon the scene, along with a couple of her friends. Something about her tone told me the kind of 'like' she was referring to. Her words stung me like a slap. I couldn't believe it, didn't want to because it was the vilest insult ever. Yuck, how could such a disgusting thing be true, I thought to myself. But it had to be, because Tinkle *didi* was thirteen, and at that age you knew everything.

I was shocked and confused, but most of all humiliated, and silently walked off to return the bike to Jagdish. I went straight home after that and my friends who had not witnessed the scene of the century couldn't understand why I left without saying bye to anyone.

At home too, I sat silently, a highly rare phenomenon. I kept replaying the scene in my head, over and over, trying to make some sense of it. Why would Bunty say something like that? Why would he like me? I didn't like him. I liked Boris Becker. Or did I like Bunty after all? I was trying to figure out if it was something I did, that elicited his unforgivable behaviour.

The next evening, Bunty kept avoiding me but I defiantly walked up to him and demanded to know why he said what he had. Right there in the playground, in front of everyone.

'It was a slip of tongue,' he replied nonchalantly, but I didn't buy that for an instant.

Things changed a lot between Bunty and me after that. We both acted normal, but never fought anymore. I tried to provoke him a few times, but he never took the bait. In fact, he largely started ignoring me. And the more distant he got, the more I found myself thinking about him. I would freeze in one corner of the playground and wonder why Bunty *bhaiyya* doesn't talk to me anymore.

Once, I sat at my study table, munching a 5-Star bar, and calculated the exact age difference between Bunty and me, as well as Boris and me. Then I walked gingerly to my mother's bedroom and asked what I thought was a very loaded question.

'How many years' difference do you have to have to get married?'

'To whom?' Mummy asked casually, not even looking up from her magazine and clearly not catching onto my guilty conscience.

'Anyone,' I tried to sound as casual as possible, but my heart was in my throat. 'How many years' difference between you and Papa?'

'Five,' she said. Five! Exactly the same as Bunty and me, I thought, and felt very happy. Boris was perhaps much too older. Satisfied, I went back to my room. But Bunty never asked me to marry him. What he did was become more and more distant, while I became increasingly lovelorn.

Accidentally, at the age of eight, I had stumbled upon the greatest romantic truth of all: Love interest is directly proportional to lack of interest from the beloved. I decided that whenever I finally met Boris Becker — needless to say once I was at least fifteen, not to mention tall, slim, blond and beautiful — I would display no interest in him at all.

Three

Supernatural

1 986 was an interesting year. We learnt through the rumour mill at school that a space shuttle exploded over the Atlantic Ocean killing seven astronauts. It was quite a sight we kids imagined; that of astronauts shot off like cannonballs, flung in all directions over an angry ocean. Even more astonishing was the news that a tunnel was being built through the sea between England and France. How would they keep the water out while building the tunnel, we wondered?

But to me, the more important developments of the year were that Boris Becker won both Wimbledon and the US Open, and that West Germany reached the finals of the football World Cup – a tournament where the Hand of God had apparently intervened and knocked England out. It was most interesting. It was also the same year that a supernatural entity decided to liven up the lives of a nondescript little government colony in central Mumbai.

Ruddy-faced and bearded, Lalit *Mamaji* was a great apostle of the good life. My mother's cousin, he was in the Navy and had moved to Mumbai a few years ago. Their drawing room always looked like it belonged in a picture book, his wife wore fashionably short hair and they always had a dog. They also had two sons, but Shiny and I were more interested in the dog. The current one was a beautiful brown Daschund called Ophelia and every time we visited them in Navy Nagar, Shiny and I would lie on the floor and rendezvous with her. Lying on the floor was essential because Ophelia had a strange habit of stationing herself under the sofa every time we visited. We adored her, and Ankush and Akshay came a distant second. They were sweet and well read, but thanks to being very cultured, not half as much fun as our Trivedi cousins. They did however, have impressive collections of books.

I was about nine and had only recently discovered books. *The Naughtiest Girl in School*, *The Wishing Chair*, *The Enchanted Forest* – I was living in Enid Blyton country. But my reading repertoire was about to expand at Ophelia's house. Both sets of parents were attending the Navy Ball, while the two boys were conveniently at some friends' place. So much to our dismay, Shiny and I were left to attend to the large, empty house, Ophelia and the prehistoric maid.

Shiny always found quick distraction with the TV, whereas I had much loftier standards than what Doordarshan could match, except when sports was on. I went to the kitchen to inspect the dinner, and returned disappointed – not a single interesting item was to be found amidst the gourds and eggplants.

A good book would save me from death by boredom, and as I was going through the bookrack I stumbled upon one called *The Wisp*. Intrigued, because I didn't know what that meant, I picked it up. The rest of the evening went by in a blur as I sank deeper and deeper into the text. I had never known a genre quite as enchanting as horror and was instantly hooked. The Wisp was a ghost that spooked a quiet little European town and all the naughty children were on its hit-list. It would appear as concentric circles of light – there were pictures in the book to illustrate just how – and if you saw such a pattern, you had better count your days. I was absolutely mesmerised. What a fabulous story! Suddenly the Wishing Chair seemed juvenile. I refused to get up even for dinner, so the maid brought my plate to me and I munched while my eyes remained glued to the pages. By the time our parents returned, looking suspiciously in high spirits, I was through with the 55-page-long book and immensely satisfied at having read such a brilliant work.

On the way back home though, I began to feel a tad unhappy. Why wasn't my life so exciting? Why hadn't I ever seen a ghost? Why wasn't there a Wisp in my colony? Then an idea struck. *Why not, indeed?*

That night, as we went to bed, I told Shiny about *The Wisp*. Despite being scared to death, she had to admit it was a very enthralling story.

'Can you imagine if the Wisp came to our colony?' I asked the pint-sized silhouette lying next to me.

'Do you think it could?' inquired Shiny, eyes shining wide, and quilt pulled up to her nose.

'Of course, why not? It can go anywhere.'

Shiny accepted that as the ultimate truth. She usually did. Anything I said with an air of authority, no matter how obtuse, was accepted without argument. And so it was with the Wisp. As I told all our friends about this awesome new creature the next day, Shiny threw in her own two bits for good measure. By the end of the clandestine conversation, I had proudly assembled a bunch of terrified five- to ten-year-olds. The fact that my first sighting came within two days didn't strike any of them as suspicious.

Late one night, around nine o'clock, Mummy suddenly had to go to Molly-Polly's for something. I seized my opportunity and begged to go along. It took us about 45 seconds to walk across to their house, but that was more than enough time for me to catch a glimpse of – God help us – The Wisp! I saw it right there on the C-Building wall, shining ominously in the moonless night. I worked on what should have been an aptly terrified expression, and just as Mummy began speaking to Yadav Uncle, I whisked Molly into a corner.

'I saw the Wisp!'

'No!' even the imperturbable Molly was horrified. 'Where?'

'On your building, on the back wall.'

'Really? What are we going to do?'

Polly, wearing her perennial grin, stole out of the bedroom to see what the excitement was about. As we related the news, the happy face instantly gave way to a look of stark fear. I thought she was about to cry, so I quickly salvaged the situation.

'Don't worry, it won't do anything to you. The Wisp is only mean to bad people.'

Comforted with the presumption that she was quite entirely good, Polly settled down. But the news spread like wildfire. All the children heard about the dreadful new entrant to the colony, and were simultaneously afraid and excited. I became something of an overnight star, being the only one to have actually seen it. More sightings followed, not all of them mine. Some of the other ambitious and imaginative children also claimed to have seen the frightful concentric rings of light. The Wisp had come to terrorise Wadala, and I had discovered the power of telling·stories.

A new ritual started among the little inhabitants of the colony. Every night from then on, a little troop of nine or ten sentries would walk around the colony after dinner, looking for the Wisp. It was great entertainment, and often we would forget about the Wisp altogether and end up making up poems and telling jokes. Other nights were more fear-inspiring, and a sizeable number would be walking around with gooseflesh. But even that excitement wore off after some days. I would lie awake at night, trying to figure out just how it could all be more authentic.

I got my answer the following week and I didn't even have to do anything. The Wisp found me. We were out on one of our night patrols, and it was just five of us that night. Molly, Polly, Pooja, Shiny and me. The darkest, creepiest corner of the colony was the backside of C-Building, flanked on two sides by the colony's mossy boundary wall. There was also a *peepul* tree there that Soni, my maid, forbade us from going near. Apparently in the villages, all ghosts lived in *peepul* trees. We weren't entirely convinced, but heeded her warnings anyway, just in case city spirits decided to follow suit. But one had to pass the C-Building corner to complete a full circle of the colony. So each time we approached the eerie spot, all of us would shut our eyes and run like mad, decelerating and breathing only after the tube-lights in front of the building became visible. I was probably one of the very few who didn't close my eyes, and that's why I saw it first. We were racing past the corner when suddenly something above our heads caught my eye. My heart froze in terror. It couldn't be! There, just below the second-floor window, was a perfectly round spot of light, arising out of absolutely nowhere.

'Look! It's the Wisp,' I whispered hoarsely, rooted to the spot in fear and astonishment.

A couple of them stopped running and came back to see what I was talking about.

'But it's not rings,' Shiny astutely observed as she peeped out from behind me, hopeful perhaps that it wasn't the Wisp after all. She was right, the Wisp was supposed to appear in concentric circles, whereas this was a full, round spot like that of a torch beam. But I was not about to give up on the thrilling discovery that my make-believe had come true. Besides, what else could it be? I asked that out loud and no one had an answer. Somebody started crying. Shiny and Polly suddenly wanted to go home. Actually, that sounded like a very good idea to me too. We were off like a shot.

'Poor Sanjana, what's going to happen to her?' asked Molly as we raced back towards the safety of our homes.

'I don't know,' I shuddered to think. It was Sanjana's bedroom window that the Wisp was lurking under.

When we returned from school the next afternoon, there was a commotion in the colony. All the aunties had converged onto the playground – a positively bizarre sight – talking in excited tones. Wondering what the matter was, I asked Soni, who had fetched the four of us from school. She said there had been a robbery. How exciting! Nothing like that had ever happened to anyone we knew, and we immediately wanted to know more.

But when Soni said 'Sanjana's house' a wave of dread rose in four little hearts. Shiny, Polly, Molly and I stared at each other bug-eyed, feeling exceptionally guilty and saying absolutely nothing.

All the grown-ups said it was the work of a thief, but we knew better. The Wisp had finally struck. It was a different matter that it never struck again and decided to leave our colony forever afterwards. No one ever saw it again and I doubt we even mentioned it after that.

Four

The House with the Horses

In 1987, double defending champion Boris Becker suffered a shocking defeat in the second round of Wimbledon and sent me into a tailspin of depression. With Becker gone, and no real interest in either Pat Cash or Ivan Lendl, I watched the men's singles final dispassionately. Eventually it was proved that hard Cash is better than Czech – as the Amul Butter hoardings proclaimed all over the city for the next few weeks. But it made no difference to my life whatsoever.

So I decided to pursue other interests for the time being. And inspired by Enid Blyton's tales, exploration came naturally. For much of that summer and a few that followed, that was all we did. The four of us – Molly, Polly, Shiny and me – were perpetually on some trail. Molly was the archetypal angel, while Polly was an imp and both were exceedingly pretty – my mother never failed to covetously point out, as if Shiny and I were supposed to do something about it. Nevertheless, ignorant of misbalanced beauty within the quartet, the four of us did everything together. We left for school together, returned singing in unison, played in the evenings and often had dinner together. And above all, we were perpetually exploring together. Anything and everything, anytime, anyplace.

We so desperately wanted a mystery to 'happen' to us that we left no stone unturned, proverbial or literal. Conveniently enough, the government colony was a hotspot for mysteries and not a square inch of the habitat was left un-investigated. But it was beyond the realms of the colony that the obsession bordered on an embarrassment for our parents. Molly's father would host a dinner at the Sea Rock Hotel to celebrate an award conferred upon him, but we would be more interested in the smuggler's party being held in the adjacent banquet hall. The grown-ups were too preoccupied to see that the obese host with the cravat and pipe was so obviously a rotten scoundrel and the ladies dripping with diamonds were surely vamps. But nothing escaped us.

We would be invited to someone's house for dinner and would go blue in the face trying to convince them that their neighbours were thieves. Often, the four of us were nowhere to be seen, only to be found under someone else's dinner table at a restaurant. Why? Because the lady's enormous handbag looked suspicious. Four little Sherlock Holmes, sticking their noses into everybody's business. It's a wonder our parents didn't send us away to a correctional facility.

It was at some obscure party that one of our greatest adventures took place. It was a fashionable gathering in a grand building with sprawling lawns – a rarity in Mumbai – and many of our parents' colleagues and their families were in attendance. The grown-ups were clearly getting up to some fishy business, because we children were hurriedly herded into an upstairs room. I was extremely upset as I had been eyeing the exotic snacks and knew well that the 'kids' room' would only be plied with insipid fare like wafers and popcorn. The telly was turned on for us.

Since India had already lost in the semi-finals of the cricket World Cup, no one was interested in watching the final between England and Australia at some Garden of Eden. So a movie called *Bond 303* – pronounced Three-Not-Three for some peculiar reason – was played to keep us occupied. I was highly affronted. If they had to contain us with a movie of all things, they should have at least checked our IQ first. As it is, it was insulting to be shepherded into a closed room, and moreover, they assumed that a preposterous Jeetendra flick would hold our interest. The nerve! I was sure there would be collective outrage and riots.

But much to my dismay all the other kids were instantly engrossed in the asinine film, even as the Jumping Jack spouted dialogue after ridiculous dialogue and did a highly unconvincing job of playing a detective. Some boys were even watching with their mouths agape. I wanted to punch them for being so vapid. Clearly, this was not the place for me, and I announced that loudly and emphatically. No one paid any attention.

I made a second announcement, 'I'm going to go explore.' This time a few ears pricked up. I had said the magic word and three figures automatically got up to follow.

We muttered something vague to the rest of the congregation, but they were not interested anyway as Parveen Babi came on for a song and dance sequence. So the four of us trudged off towards the door directly opposite to the one we had been shunted in from.

As we shut the door behind us, there was total darkness. Pitch black. Polly immediately felt scared but after a few reassuring words her courage returned. We took a few steps blindly, groping about for walls or anything else to hold onto. As our eyes were slowly adjusting to the dark, Shiny bumped into something, something huge, and let out a muffled scream. But the silhouette didn't budge. It stood absolutely still, looming enormously above our heads. Gradually, we could make out a shape – a horse's head, gigantic and larger than life.

'Is it a dead horse?' someone inquired and I felt a shiver down my spine.

'Let's find the light quickly,' I suggested and all of us went off in different directions, arms stretched out and stumbling.

Molly found the switches and instantly the room was flooded with light. A grand old crystal chandelier hung down from a vaulted ceiling and shone directly above the most beautiful sculpture we had ever seen. It was enormous, even intimidating. A shining, ebony-black bust of a horse, mounted on an exquisite pedestal of rosewood and ivory. We forgot to breathe and stood there slack-jawed, looking up at the beast that dwarfed us by at least three feet.

'It's a statue,' a relieved Polly informed everyone with a grin, just in case we still hadn't got the picture.

I shifted my gaze and it landed on another horse. This time it was a beautiful brown stallion, galloping wild. It was oil on canvas, on the far wall. Beneath it, on a glass table was a smaller wood carving of two horses, rising up to neigh.

'There are horses everywhere!' Molly exclaimed and we spun around in a daze.

On the centre table immediately to our left, a marble horse head stared up at us. Dozens of horse paintings, large and small, hung on every wall. For some reason the place gave us the creeps. We decided we had had enough of horses and ran for the next door, neglecting to switch off the lights.

The next room was a large, airy hall with what looked like a gigantic centipede in the centre. Upon inspection it revealed itself to be a million-seater dining table. We had never seen anything like it – a glass-top, supported on four belligerent, bronze war-horses. We stopped short at the door itself. It was like being in one of those nightmares where no matter where you run, the monster always reaches first. Rooted, we scanned the rest of the hall out of the corner of our eyes, as light glimmered in from the room behind us. One wall was dressed with large, heavily curtained French windows, while the opposite one showed off yet another enormous painting. This one was a herd of white unicorns. And on the mantelpiece on the far side was a whole army of miniature horses. The four of us stood in a silent line, our shadows forty-feet-tall against an eerie yellow background.

'Why does this house have only horses, Da?' Shiny whispered, always the one to ask questions. She seemed rather upset though, and was holding onto my arm. I was at a loss for words. I motioned for everyone to go through the door on our right, and the investigators trudged along reluctantly.

But it was all the same: Hall after hall of countless horse paintings, sculptures and figurines. We went up a flight of stairs, and through more than half a dozen rooms, including two bedrooms. But we only encountered horses everywhere. It just didn't make any sense, and in my book that meant 'suspicious' straightaway. Polly and Shiny were quite petrified by then, and meekly suggested we turn back and return to the safety of Bond Three-Not-Three.

'No,' I said with an authority that belied the gooseflesh on my arms. 'We have to find out what's going on.' So further we went, to find out just what was going on.

As we opened a double door, we were hit by a blast of cool air. The night sky loomed ahead of us and we found ourselves on some sort of walkway, open on both sides and connecting two buildings. It was quite unexpected, and we were thankful to be in the open, away from all the mysterious horses.

'It's a bridge.' Polly had a great flair for stating the obvious, although her vocabulary was slightly off the mark sometimes.

'Should we go further?' inquired the ever-sensible Molly, looking in my direction. But I had a reputation to protect, so despite desperately wanting to sprint back, I found myself saying, 'No, let's just see what's there in that building and then we can go back.' No one agreed, but no one said no. We walked cautiously along and spoke in hushed tones for reasons we didn't understand. Music drifted in from somewhere, a vague reminder that we were still on the same planet as the party was.

The walkway was suspended on the first- or second-floor level. Twenty feet ahead, it ended into a floor-landing and a staircase went up and down the building. Light filtered in from a couple of floors above, while below us the stairs disappeared into a cavernous black. Under normal circumstances, the brave investigators would have opted to explore the dark, but we had exhibited enough bravery for one day, so we chose to follow the light.

On the next floor-landing there was just a heavy door, ominously padlocked, and nothing else. We carried on up. This time, we reached a corridor, with a number of doors down one side and an open railing on the other. At the far end was a dainty white iron gate, not much higher than we were. And beyond it was an open-air space and the source of the lights. Like moths to a flame, we walked on in a stupor. Nobody spoke a word until we reached the gate.

It was a pool deck, with lit lampposts all around. We pressed our faces against the open-worked grill and peered in. The 25-metre swimming pool was dry like a desert.

'Why isn't there any water in the pool?' Shiny wanted to know, eyes wide and her incisors protruding out further than usual.

'It's probably haunted.' I was compulsive. I loved building up an atmosphere and didn't mind throwing in a bit of horror with a mystery. Three pairs of eyes widened and peered in even more intently.

'I don't want to go there,' Polly whined.

Oh! Now there was an idea. I hadn't even considered the possibility of jumping the gate. Now I did.

'Nothing will happen. I'm sure there's something suspicious there and I'm going to see what it is. Molly, come with me.'

Molly didn't look like she wanted to join me in the least bit, but she started climbing the gate just the same. It was surprisingly easy, and we hauled ourselves over and down without much trouble. We had gone only a couple of steps when the two tots suddenly realised that they were alone and separated from us by wrought-iron grills.

'We're coming too!' they wailed.

A few minutes later, all four of us were standing alongside the diving board, staring at the blue floor-tiles in amazement, as if a deserted swimming pool was just about the most arresting sight in the world. Several whispered explanations were offered.

'Maybe it's a false floor and they hide smuggled goods down there,' I said. 'That's why they can't have water.'

'Maybe they hide weapons in it.'

'Maybe they kill people and bury them underneath.'

There was always an unspoken competition to see who could come up with the most morbid and shocking theory.

'What is that, up there?' asked Shiny, pointing to the diving platform looming ominously above our heads like a cement-and-iron beast.

'It's for platform diving,' I announced, always smug in exhibiting my savoir-faire. 'And this one here,' I said, pointing to the edge of the pool, 'is called a springboard. It's like jelly when you jump on it.'

We were debating whether or not we would have the courage to dive off the platform when suddenly a booming voice from behind startled us.

'Oye! *Kaun hai?*' a voice bellowed. We jumped out of our skins and turned around in panic. A large ogre of a man with appalling buckteeth was shouting and charging heavily towards us from the far side of the deck. We all screamed and ran for our lives. He came running after us. We didn't even dare look back as we raced towards the gate. We could hear his footsteps getting closer and him yelling.

'*Kya kar rahe ho? Abhi batata hoon, badmash!*'

We could only imagine what a villain like that would do if he indeed got his hands on us. He would kill us, that was for sure. Just think how angry our parents would be with us, then. We reached the gate and I practically vaulted over it in an instant, despite all my thirty-five kilos. I turned around to see the thug less than fifty metres from the gate.

'Hurry!' I screamed at the top of my lungs as Shiny scrambled over, followed by Molly. Polly quickly started climbing on next, but just as she was straddling onto our side, she slipped and slid back. He was almost there.

'Mummyyyyyyyyy!' Polly wailed, dangling awkwardly on the wrong side of the gate, and seemingly giving up the fight for her life. The monster was almost there, five more strides and he would be able to sink his claws into Polly. Eight-year-old Molly and nine-year-old me had never felt such responsibility and fear.

Instinctively, we stuck our arms through the grill and pushed Polly's legs upwards. Just in the nick of time, her weight shifted and an instant later she tumbled onto our side, head over heels, her frilly pink and white party frock turning inside out over her head like an umbrella. The brute was at the gate, grunting, but out of reach. We weren't going to take any chances though. Any minute now, he was going to whip out a gun. Pulling Polly off the floor we turned and ran at top speed.

Halfway down the corridor, I looked back to see him hurling a granade at us. I yelled out the warning. We all shut our eyes and ran faster than we could ever have imagined possible, just as a shoe went whizzing past us and over the railing to our right. His angry howls diminished as we raced down the stairs, our hearts in our mouths. We didn't stop until we reached the very bottom of the stairs and it was only then that we realised we had missed the walkway back to safety.

'What should we do now?' asked Molly, bent over and catching her breath.

'Should we go back up to the bridge?' I panted in response.

Polly was crying full-throttle. 'I'm not going back there,' she managed to wail in between sobs.

'Da please, let's not go back up,' Shiny pleaded, also looking on the verge of tears.

I was terrified myself and didn't know what to do. I looked around. We were standing on the grass, under the open sky. The lawns stretched all around the vast grounds. There was no light where we were and we trooped off in the vast darkness, walking against the wind, as trees cast dancing shadows on the grass beneath our feet.

We carried on encircling the colossal building. Polly was crying and Shiny was near delirium, harping on about what would happen if we never found the party. And then suddenly, it was there. Round the corner and barely a hundred yards ahead of us was the grand entrance with the fountains, where we had first arrived with our parents. We ran towards it, thanking God and screaming with relief and laughing and sobbing. Past the fountain, the foyer and into the main hall we ran, where the party was on in full swing. We scampered past various trousers and saris, until we found familiar ones and dashed to snuggle with security.

But we didn't get the heroes' reception that we so thoroughly deserved. Just a few quick hugs and then pointless, dimwit questions like 'Why aren't you watching the movie?' 'Do you know that Australia has won the World Cup?' Hullo? Did anyone even hear what we just said? I mean, here were four little kids looking like they'd just climbed out of hell, ranting about crooks and murderers and no one seemed to register one word. They all just looked very amused and in ridiculously high spirits. Thankfully, at last Polly's father lifted the sobbing girl into his arms and asked her why she was crying.

'Because that man tried to kill me,' she said and started bawling again, perhaps at the comprehension of what she had just endured.

'Which man?' he asked, but he was smiling.

'The man in the swimming pool,' she said, rubbing her eyes. But instead of immediately calling a search party and hunting down the criminals, Yadav uncle planted a big kiss on her cheek and then proceeded to try and feed her a kebab. Were grown-ups insane? We spent the rest of the party moping about in the hall, refusing to leave our parents' side for an instant. And from then on, we always eyed poor horses with suspicion.

Five

The Pump House Smugglers

The top-secret meetings used to be held in C-15. Five o'clock sharp. Everyone had to knock three times and then say the password. The password would be changed every week for security purposes. Strictly no entry for outsiders. And of course, you had to wear the badge; otherwise, even legitimate members would be denied entry.

After all, we were a top-of-the-line investigation team: The Secret Seven. So what if we had borrowed the name from Enid Blyton? It didn't matter that this was suburban Mumbai and not an English village. And really, it was inconsequential that instead of lemonade served in the fictional meetings, we drank 'Rasna' by the gallon. What mattered was that we were the real deal, not mere characters in a book.

The idea was borne out of boredom, during one particularly dull summer. We had done everything in our capacity to keep ourselves engaged, including a fancy-dress competition and a sell-out dance performance for all the parents. Wimbledon had come and gone and a new West German named Steffi Graf had taken up residence in my heart alongside Boris Becker, who had disappointed me yet again by losing the final to one prissy-looking Stefan Edberg.

The annual colony-picnic to Aksa beach was over and done with. We had even discovered a witch in the adjacent colony, who kept a white parrot in a gilded cage in her balcony. The spectacular bird could make human conversation and it would screech out 'Hello! How are you?' across the boundary wall to us, whenever we played *chor-police*, up on the water tanks. We tried in vain to rescue the poor creature from the clutches of the old hag, who was undoubtedly fattening him up to be eaten later.

Everything had been exhausted, so we resigned ourselves to books. And books, back then, meant only Enid Blyton. I had graduated from *The Magic Faraway Tree* to more mature literature, thanks to my father's summer holiday gift – the entire collection of the 'Secret Seven' volumes. And for a week after Papa came home with that large cardboard carton, I was invisible and inaudible around the house and the colony. I wouldn't even go out to play when the rest of the children came calling and they all thought I had developed some mysterious illness. Eventually though the entire work was exhausted, all sixteen of them. And boredom hit like an avalanche. I seriously considered writing to Enid Blyton, hoping to persuade her to continue, spin a few more yarns. But to my dismay, I learnt that Blyton had died the year after she travelled to India to visit the maharani of Jaipur. Apparently all the little princesses who were studying at Her Royal Highness' school in 1967 had been lucky enough to meet Enid Blyton in person. I couldn't believe it.

'You are so lucky!' I exclaimed enviously to my mother. 'You got meat loaf for dinner, had a swimming pool and even got to meet Enid Blyton – why don't you send *me* there?'

'It's not the same anymore. I believe the girls even eat in steel plates now,' she said with a sudden shudder of revulsion.

Finally, as always, we decided to do something about our boredom ourselves, self-reliant little lot that we were. The Secret Seven legacies would live on, we decided, in our neighbourhood. The first task was to identify the exalted seven. The four founding members obviously gained automatic entry – Molly, Polly, Shiny and me. The task was to identify the other three. Pooja and Dimple were desperate to join, but we wouldn't hear of it. The original Secret Seven had three girls, and we already had four. Besides, both were sissies. The other three members just *had* to be boys. Monty, the rowdiest boy in the neighbourhood and the podgy, mild-mannered Sunny came through a process of natural selection, being our best friends among the boys. But one vacancy remained.

Competition became hotter than a presidential race as word spread about the exclusive club. The six existing members became the most popular people in the neighbourhood: indulged, pampered, and flattered. Since it was evident that I was largely the decision maker, some of the kids even brought me a lollypop or a chocolate everyday – sycophancy and corruption at grass-root level.

Shiny would have loved to include Chintu, who was now known as Kapil, but he was too dense, and even though 15-year-old Bunty Bhaiyya was an impressive campaigner, he was simply too old. The search went on for days until Molly suggested Venkatesh.

Venkatesh was a quiet, inconspicuous South Indian boy who always had some white powder on his forehead, studied a lot and came out to play for exactly one hour by the clock. But he was smart and we all knew that. He read encyclopaedias as a hobby, had memorised the classification of dinosaurs and always ranked first in class. Other than the fact that we barely knew him, he fit the bill perfectly.

He lasted exactly a week. He never quit officially, but just stopped showing up. We barely even noticed and continued to pretend we were seven.

'He's busy studying today.'

'He's not feeling well.'

But we never said 'he quit,' because that would have been utter ignominy. Why would anyone relinquish such an honour? All desperate pleas to replace Venkatesh fell on deaf ears. Bunty Bhaiyya and Sunny's elder brother Bunny would bang outside Molly-Polly's bedroom window even as our meetings were in progress. They poked fun at our 'SS' badges calling it 'Social Service.' They also told us that Social Service was what people who swept the streets did. You can imagine it didn't go down very well with us. Fat chance of them being inducted.

Protocol would be maintained strictly at the meetings. Molly would bring glasses of Rasna and jam-filled biscuits, because even the maid wasn't allowed entry. Then, a quick check on any unusual sightings or whiffs of a mystery. Each one by turn would suggest a potential case and Molly would meticulously jot down notes in our SS Diary. Most of the time we cooked up stories and went around the colony with magnifying glasses, binoculars and what have you, pretending to be hot on some trail. But sometimes we smelled a real mystery.

The monument being constructed on what was once the beloved badminton court was finished well before the holidays were over. I demanded to know what on earth the monstrosity was.

'Why have they made a building on the baddy court?' I asked my mother. 'Is someone going to live in there?'

'Don't be silly!' she said while frying some dubious-looking vegetable. 'It's a pump house.'

'What's a pump house?' I was incredulous, never having heard of such a thing.

'It's going to make our water supply better.'

'What's wrong with our water now?' I had to get to the bottom of this.

Exasperated, she turned around and said, 'There *is* a problem. You don't know anything!'

You don't know anything was mother-speak for 'conversation over, get out of here'. I took my cue and beat a hasty retreat.

But outside, I told the whole world about it.

'That's a Pump house you know,' I said to a congregation of about fifteen children. 'They're going to do something with our water supply.'

'Are they going to poison us?' Polly inquired. All the investigators were well trained to ask questions, even the youngest ones.

'I don't know, but we could find out,' I said and five pairs of eyes gleamed. The Secret Seven, or rather Six, had found their next case.

That night after dinner, all of us scampered out of our homes and assembled in front of the grand pumphouse. It was very dark, there were no lights, no sound and all of us stood in silence for a while, not quite sure what to do next. Finally, someone suggested we try to go inside. A few members were reluctant, but wouldn't say so. That would have been social humiliation. We tiptoed our way around to the main entrance, a large, double-door painted blue. It didn't have a padlock on, and when we pushed, it wouldn't budge.

'It's locked,' someone noted.

'But there is no lock,' Shiny pointed out, waving away mosquitoes, her ponytail bobbing in the moonlight.

'Maybe they have some hi-fi locking system,' monkey-like Monty suggested. We all had to agree.

'Let's try the windows,' I said. Enid Blyton's characters would have done that. They simply never accepted failure or gave up on an investigation.

Round the bend we went and came upon a large window that was too high for any of us. Sunny did the gallant thing and offered his stout back. He went down on all fours, and one by one each of us climbed on to peer inside. There was nothing except pitch black. We couldn't see a thing, but everyone wanted their turn nevertheless. Suddenly Molly exclaimed.

'There's some light coming out of the ground!'

What? All of a sudden there was too much excitement and everyone tried to climb onto Sunny simultaneously. It didn't work and we all tumbled. Sunny refused to offer his back anymore. But we had to see the light that was coming out of the ground. I settled things by being autocratic, the only foolproof method, always.

'I am the leader and I am going to see first.' Sunny went back down and I quickly scrambled up. And what I saw was even stranger than what Molly had described. There was not just a beam of light, but the silhouette of *a man* emerging from underground!

'Holy Moly! There's a man coming out of the ground! He has a torch in his hand,' I gave them all a running commentary. 'He's just floating upwards. Now he's standing and he's got a bag in his hand. He's looking down and seems to be talking to someone.'

Just then another head started to emerge from the ground. This was all just too much. I realised I should let the others see the improbable sight. Everyone went up for a few seconds and gasped as they saw the second silhouette emerge from terra firma. Sunny also finally got a chance to peek in as I offered my back.

'What's going on now?' I asked him from underneath, panting from having to bear his considerable weight.

'I think they are looking at me,' he squeaked, a bit unsure.

'What!' I straightened up and literally threw him off my back. We could see light on the windowpane now.

'*Kaun hai wahan*!' Suddenly a voice yelled out from inside. We stared at each other in fright.

'RUN!' Polly screamed at her fellow investigators and our legs instantly followed her instruction. But we were too late. Just as we started to race off, one of the men came flying out of the large blue door and charged towards us. But on seeing us, he stopped short.

'*Bachhey hain*,' he called out, seemingly to his partner, who was still inside. They're just children, he had said. Little did he know.

Then he turned back to us and bellowed, '*Kya chahiye tumko? Kya kar rahe ho?*'

'What are *you* doing here?' I shouted back at him, putting up a brave face, arms akimbo. Taken aback, he said he was doing his work.

'What work? Nobody works at night except smugglers,' Monty informed him. Clearly, Monty was right because the minute he said that, the man started charging at us again. We ran for our lives.

'Come back here!' he shouted from behind us. 'I'll show you what work I can do!'

The same nocturnal activity went on for a few weeks. Sometimes we would see them arrive and disappear inside for half an hour or so. At other times, we would reach just as they were leaving and they would angrily chase us halfway to our homes. Some nights, they didn't show up at all, probably wary of the fact that they were being watched. And there were instances when only one of them came instead of two.

But they always carried a shady-looking canvas bag, always disappeared underground and emerged with the torch in hand. Finally, we decided we had to notify our parents about the nefarious activity going on practically in our backyard. We had to do it *en masse* for it to be taken seriously. So we waited till one evening when Molly-Polly's father was having tea with Papa at our house, watching a news report about the Olympics in some far-off land called Seoul. Apparently someone named Ben Johnson had to return his gold medal because he was a druggie. What did that have to do with running fast, I wondered as the six of us filed into the living room.

'We have to tell you something,' Molly and I announced jointly.

'Sure, what is it?' Both fathers looked keenly interested, but Mummy ignored our existence as she went about her chores.

'But first, you have to promise that you'll believe us,' I said, a little sceptical of their interest. Usually they didn't take us seriously, no matter how grave a problem we reported. When they nodded acceptance with big smiles, we proceeded to tell them the whole story. As we finished, Shiny urged my father to react, as he should.

'Papa, you're a government officer. You'll catch the smugglers, won't you?'

'*Beta*, they are not smugglers,' he patiently explained to all of us, amid chuckles. 'They are doing their job of installing the machinery in the pump house.'

'Then why do they go underground?' We all appealed. This was going to end in disaster.

'Because that is where the water is,' Papa clarified. 'Underground.'

'But why do they work only at night?' I asked, refusing to end the matter there.

Aha! That one had even our fathers stumped.

'You'll have to ask them that.' Yadav Uncle offered, with a hearty laugh.

What kind of a senseless, inadequate answer was that? I wished I were an adult. I would have arrested them immediately. The smugglers, not the fathers.

But the pump-house Smugglers were never arrested. They eventually finished whatever questionable business they were up to and after that we only saw them sporadically, perhaps once in two or three months. What a waste of an admirable investigation it was.

The Secret Seven disbanded after that. It was just too heartbreaking.

Six

View From a Tree Top

It was well past ten at night. A crisp breeze swirled around and dim light emanated from a few scattered windows. Julian, Anne, George and Timmy cautiously made their way up to Owl's Dene. Dick was ill, and had to miss out on the adventure, much to his dismay. The neighbourhood was awfully quiet, but somewhere at the end of the lane someone was watching TV at an offensively loud volume. It was enough to ruin the well-orchestrated mood, but the Famous Five ploughed along all the same, towards the sinister Owl's Dene.

A few hushed words were exchanged as they came upon D-II/66. Timmy, who was threatening to surge ahead, was brought to a halt. Sure enough, just as speculated, that sole first-floor window was the source of cacophony in the area.

'Had to be them,' Julian noted with a disapproving shake of the head.

'I told you,' George responded in a signature smug tone. 'Let's throw a stone at the window.'

'Oh don't do that!' Anne looked aghast. 'What if someone sees us?'

The debate went on for a few moments and then they decided to trudge back. After all, there were parents waiting at home, and in George's case, homework was still to be done. George grabbed Timmy by the handle and reversed direction.

Timmy was the bicycle. Shiny was Anne, Meha Srivatsa was the scholarly Julian and Dick was always absconding simply because there wasn't anyone to play the fourth role. I, quite naturally, was George.

The government colony in Kidwai Nagar in Delhi was a child's worst nightmare. After a glorious five years in Mumbai, Papa had been transferred back to Delhi for a short, two-year posting, and Shiny and I were bordering on clinical depression. Wadala had been Lilliputian Land; our new colony in Delhi was like Gulliver's revenge – the entire child population had been wiped out. Shiny and I had no one to play with. There had been brief excitement during that particular fortnight of the summer, with Steffi Graf and Boris Becker making it an all-German Wimbledon that year, my entire family of four glued to the television each evening. But that too had passed and there was absolutely nothing to do. And so, I fell hopelessly into the bottomless pit that books can sometimes be. I was too old for Secret Seven now, so the Famous Five it had to be.

The Famous Five's Georgina Kirrin presented a much-needed solution. I had always been tomboyish without giving much thought to it – I played *chor-police* instead of dolls and preferred football to the dimwit game of 'house-house'. And it had never been an issue until recently, when on my twelfth birthday Papa gifted me my gleaming new, red racing bicycle. A boy's bike – I was delighted!

'She's growing up now,' my mother admonished Papa as he unveiled the present. 'Why do you keep encouraging this stupid, boyish behaviour? At least you could have bought her a proper ladies' cycle!' She slapped her forehead in frustration and stormed off, even as I hopped on to test the baby.

But from then on, I began to notice that my mother made it a point to try and make me conform. She said 'weird girls' like me would grow up to be lonely because no boy wanted to marry another boy. 'Nice girls should wear skirts and speak softly, not yell about in shorts and a mud-caked face,' she would tell me.

I *really* enjoyed yelling about in shorts and a mud-caked face. So I didn't really know what to do about my peculiar situation until Papa introduced me to Georgina Kirrin – a girl after my own heart. Apparently, she had simply decided to become a boy. That was it. I couldn't believe how simple it was. All I had to do was announce that I'm going to be a boy, and everyone would treat me as one. Of course, the problem of marrying Boris Becker would have to be dealt with when the situation presented itself.

Pompously I strode into a men's barbershop and asked for a 'boy-cut'. I gave away all my skirts and dresses to children in the servants' quarters behind our row of houses and informed my parents that they had acquired a son. My father was mildly amused. Mummy hit the roof, but I couldn't care less. I had found my calling. From then on I referred to myself as a boy, wore only shorts or jeans, forced Shiny to address me as 'Bhaiyya' and generally made a song and dance about being a boy. Ladies at dinner parties would ask my mother what her son's name was. My mother would wail in despair but I would swell with pride.

But despite my dramatic sex change, Shiny and I continued to be friendless. The only companions we had were the servants' children and we happily invited a whole bunch of them to our backyard every day to play football or seven stones. We even tried buying a dog. In fact the buying was easy – we simply had to ask our grandfather Gashaji for the dough. It was the keeping that turned out to be a problem. Mummy threatened that it would be either her or the dog in the house. The choice was painfully obvious to Shiny and me, but Papa wouldn't hear of living without his wife. And so the dog was promptly sold back. Needless to say, we had christened him Timmy for the few days that he was with us. A Pomeranian would have done an infinitely better job of playing Timmy, than my bicycle ever could.

We may never have found Julian either if I hadn't been trying to build a tree house one weekend afternoon. I was perched halfway up the rather frail *gulmohar* tree in our front lawn and was trying to nail in two planks of wood. That was the tree house in its entirety – two planks for two people to park on. With my limited carpentry skills, I could not have embarked on a more ambitious project.

And soon, from my newly-built lookout, I had an exclusive aerial view into our neighbours' gardens. Many of them were shabbily maintained compared to ours and there wasn't much to catch my eye, but all of a sudden, just when I was about to lose interest I saw the impossible. In the house next but one to ours, a lady was inspecting a barren flower bed and accompanying her was, could my eyes be deceiving me, a girl who seemed to be about the same age as me. I almost fell off the tree in excitement.

'Hello! Hello!' I shouted at the top of my voice. 'Up here! Look up here.'

The girl and her mother squinted up into the sky and instantly found me waving my arms about like a chimpanzee. The spindly, bespectacled girl looked as though she didn't have the least bit of interest in making my acquaintance and immediately darted for indoors, but her mother restrained her and tried to hold a conversation with me.

'Do you live in that house?' she asked. The absurdity of grown-ups never failed to astound me. Live in the house, as opposed to what? The tree? But I thought the better of pointing that out to her.

'Yes I do. My name is Tanya. What's your name, I mean your daughter's?'

'This was Meha, my daughter. I thought you were a boy!' the lady responded, instantly altering my dim opinion of her.

'Oh, thank you!' I shouted back. 'When did you move into this house?'

'Why don't you come down from the tree and we can meet properly?'

Yes, not a bad idea. I quickly scrambled back down and ran out of the front gate. Meha's mother had to literally drag her out of their house, and the girl looked like she was about to cry. When she realised it was too late as I was already at their fence, she went limp and avoided eye contact.

'Hi Meha,' I said in my friendliest, chirpiest voice. 'I'm Tanya.'

'Hi,' she managed to mumble, looking suspiciously out of the corner of her eye.

I quickly told Meha's mother how Shiny and I had searched the entire colony for someone our age and come up with zilch. It was great to have met Meha now, I added. Mrs Srivatsa, Meha's mother, then proceeded to properly introduce herself and her family. They also had an elder daughter who was in college while Meha here apparently did not believe in venturing out hunting for friends.

'We did see some children playing in your backyard yesterday, but we thought they were all boys and so Meha didn't want to make friends with anyone,' she said with a smile.

Shiny had meanwhile stepped out to see what the commotion was about and was thrilled when her eyes found Meha. Needless to say, the pony-tailed girl's arrival seemed to soothe Meha's nerves and she instantly seemed more sociable. Soon we discovered that Meha was an avid bookworm herself: more importantly, she devoured Enid Blyton. And thus began a great friendship.

For many months the three of us rode my bicycle in turns, stole guavas, enacted Famous Five dramas and discovered the joys of renting video cassettes from the shady little shop in the flea market. A few months after Meha, Shiny and me had solidified into an inseparable threesome, our new neighbours arrived.

'You know, I saw a new family moving into D-II/66 in the morning,' Mother said distractedly, while trying to help Shiny with her alphabets. 'Maybe you should go see if they have children your age.'

'Okay!' I sat up straight, ever-eager.

'Oh, I don't mean right this very minute,' she said. 'Your father will be home soon and we have something to tell you.'

Uh-oh. This better not be something completely dreadful like the news of a baby sister or brother coming along soon. One of my classmates at school had recently been delivered this knockout punch by her parents, after keeping her guessing for months. Poor thing had thought all along that she was about to receive a pony for her birthday.

'What is it?' I asked, very suspicious.

'Well, it's some very good news but let Papa come home and then we'll all talk about it,' she said, grinning so wide that I was suddenly sure there was something undoubtedly dubious in store.

'What is it!' I jumped up and demanded, alarmed to the bone. 'I want to know right now!'

It was either the look of genuine distress on my face or the fact that she was having trouble containing herself in any case, that my mother uncharacteristically decided to divulge then and there.

'Your father has been posted to Hong Kong,' she said with a flourish as though we were expected to break into a jig upon hearing the words.

'Hong Kong, where's that?' all three asked in unison. I knew vaguely that it was some place outside India, but why would anyone want to live anywhere other than India? Why was mother looking so oddly thrilled about it? This was terrible news. I was due to be the head girl of my school in exactly six years' time. What would happen to those plans?

'It's a wonderful island country off the coast of China,' mother informed us, still unable to retract the corners of her mouth from near her ears.

'Will we have to speak Chinese there?' It was now Shiny's turn to be truly horrified.

'Oh God, no,' she said, instantly frustrated that we weren't able to appreciate how 'wonderful' a piece of news it was. 'It's a British colony; you'll get along fine with English. And it's a great opportunity for your father. He'll be paid in Hong Kong dollars and we'll even be able to buy a fancy car.'

That virtual buyoff settled it for the moment. And our attention and conversation turned back to the new family in the block. Later that same evening, we saw two girls helping their parents move cartons from the truck into the house; one girl was about our age, while the younger one may have been about six, too young to hold our interest. By now, Meha had turned into as keen a friend-hunter as Shiny and me and we scoped them out from a distance at first.

Mummy urged us to go and make friends with them. They're such 'beautiful girls', she would say, as if such inconsequentialities mattered in life. Could they ride bikes? Did they watch tennis or read Enid Blyton? That was the question. Eventually, despite the newcomers looking a bit stuffy, the Famous Three marched across to D-II/66.

'Hello, what nice children you are!' The impeccably attired mother beamed at us and we wondered why. 'Come in and meet Rekha and Gaurika,' she said.

The first round of pleasantries wasn't over yet when trouble started. I had just introduced myself.

'Why do you look like a boy?' Rekha, the elder one, giggled.

'Because I am one,' I stated matter-of-factly.

'No, Tanya is a girl's name,' the mother added, with a touch of condescension.

Shiny and Meha rolled their eyes – they had been witness to such conversations on innumerable occasions.

'Yes, I know,' I said, mildly irritated. 'I used to be a girl, but now I am a boy.'

'That's not possible!' Rekha and Gaurika burst out laughing, and to add insult to injury, the mother added, 'What rubbish. How can you become a boy?'

I could feel embarrassment running hot through my cheeks and ears. 'It is *not* rubbish!' I shot back. My father had never questioned my decision, so who was she? As if reading my thoughts, Aunty snapped, 'What's wrong with you? Haven't your parents taught you any manners?'

'Haven't your parents taught *you* any?' I asked of her, immediately ashamed of my unforgivable rudeness. That did it. I thought she was going to hit me and I suddenly didn't know what to do. Better get out of here, I told myself. And before another word could be spoken, I ran back out the door. Like a coward. I felt terrible – one couldn't talk to an aunty like that. Eventually, Shiny and Meha joined me on the playground, amazingly enough, with Rekha and Gaurika in tow.

From then on, we did sort of become friends with the two sisters, but needless to say, their mother didn't dote upon me. She objected to almost everything I did. Like the day when on my suggestion, we decided to play football. Rekha went home crying to her mother because she would have rather played with Barbie. Aunty stormed out onto the playground and bellowed that girls don't play 'disgusting games' like football.

And that's how it went until the dam burst. Aunty didn't know that we often invited the servants' children to play with us in our backyard. I didn't even realise it could be an issue until one day when we encouraged all the kids to come out and play in the main central park of the block. That evening, instead of the few scattered children spotted daily on the playground, there was an absolute besiege. And it was such fun. We played cricket, seemingly hundreds of us – the Famous Three, my visiting cousins, all the servants' children from the entire block, and of course, Rekha and Gaurika. I was near delirious with all the action and in no mood to meet the unfriendly neighbourhood aunty. But there she was, all of a sudden, just when I had latched onto an incredible catch, screaming and darting our way across the playground like a rocket with extra fuel. Uh oh. What had I done now? For the first few moments I couldn't even understand what she was saying. I fearfully looked up at the loony lady now towering above me, waving her hands angrily.

'. . . how dare you? My daughters are *not* going to play with these disgusting servants! Where is your mother? I want to speak to your mother, you horrible child!' Her bright red lipstick enunciating every word and making her look all the more menacing. The words registered in my mind in slow motion as I was too spellbound by the quivering crimson mouth.

Deathly silence all around. Nobody spoke or even moved. I shifted about uncomfortably, but before I could think of an appropriate response, she took me by surprise as she grabbed me by the collar and started dragging me in the general direction of my house, hollering all the while.

I was well and truly terrified. I had no idea how my mother would react. I was hoping she wouldn't even let the screaming banshee into the house. I was wrong – as soon as Mummy saw me cowering at one end of the Mad Lady's arm, her puzzled expression transformed into a very stern one. Oh boy, the end was near. My mother was the strictest disciplinarian on the planet. She was like Edward Scissor-hands when it came to cutting us down to size. What was in store for me?

But as soon as she grasped what the entire ruckus was about, Mummy's face changed again. Now, an expression of exasperation began to form and it seemed to be directed at Aunty, not me! When Madame Nuts was finished, my mother spoke quietly, dripping with the sarcasm that Shiny and I recognised so well.

'You don't want your girls to play with the servant's children?' she asked and Aunty clearly missed the tone of voice, as she was quick to reply, 'Of course!'

'But why?' asked Mum. 'Isn't it better to have many friends than to have none?'

My adversary's IQ can be gauged from the fact that she still didn't catch on to which side my mother was quite unmistakably on.

'But they're all filthy and diseased!' she was almost pleading now. 'How can you let your own daughters play with them?'

'They can handle a few germs. It's all a part of childhood, don't you think?' Mummy asked, the fakest smile in the world drawn across her face. 'If you don't want your daughters playing with them, keep them away by all means. But I don't see what that has to do with my children. I'm sure they don't force anyone to play with them.'

Finally, Aunty got the point. She whimpered, looked like she was about to start again but then thought the better of it. In the end she conceded defeat with a shrug of the shoulder and an indecipherable mumble, which sounded like 'Your wish' or something equally dense, and slumped out of the house.

'Now what are you waiting for?' Mummy said to me with a stern face, but frolic in her voice and eyes, 'Go back out and play.'

And I ran back out feeling on top of the world.

Seven

City of Angels

He was an angel. I knew it the minute I saw him. He walked into the classroom, with a pink-and-grey sports bag slung over one shoulder, a brilliant halo of light emanating all around him. Mesmerising. I had never set eyes on an angel before, having seen them only in paintings and postcards. And he was literally picture-perfect: tall, athletic, soft blond wisps of hair on his forehead, and the most heavenly smile this side of the stratosphere. He was an angel in flesh, and I was the new kid in Hong Kong's Blue Isle School.

In May 1990, my father was sent on a deputation posting to Hong Kong, one of the most glamorous cities of the world, and our lives changed dramatically and irreversibly. Unaware that I would eventually find angels inhabiting it, I serendipitously exclaimed at touchdown, 'This is like paradise!'

Everything, from that surreal landing on a sea-strip to the chrome-and-glass skyscrapers, was overwhelming. The city centre – Admiralty, Queensway Plaza and Central – was packed with people of all races, designer showrooms, restaurants, clubs and offices. It was breathtaking. But above all, it was the natural beauty of the island nation that astonished me. Beyond the city centre, the winding roads went past vast expanses of deep blue sea, gorgeous beaches, lush vegetation-covered hills, and almost like a paradox, high-rise residential buildings rising out of seemingly nowhere.

We were to live in Baguio Villas, a condominium complex away from the city, facing the open ocean. There was a swimming pool, a tennis court and a golf driving range. Until then I had only fantasised about such an existence. My despondency at having to leave India was short-lived. There wasn't much to miss except Gashaji and my cousins, as school life in Delhi had been a real drag. And our parents assured us that our grandfather and cousins would visit often.

Shiny and I were to study in a British school, which meant the school term wouldn't start until September. But two months ahead, we had to take an entrance exam to make sure our English was satisfactory. Papa drove us to Blue Isle School one morning, and it was love at first sight. It was a terraced structure built along the slope of a hill, and looked more like a resort than school. It had three basketball courts – back in India we would have been lucky to have one – an indoor gym-cum-hockey field, a 50-metre swimming pool with spectator seating, four tennis courts, two squash courts and one full-size football ground. Just when we joyfully thought there may not be any classrooms at all, we came upon them – cheerful, painted hues of yellow, red, purple and blue. Mr David Jones, the affable principal showed us around and ended the tour at the uniform shop.

'The girls wear navy skirts with blue-striped shirts,' he told us brightly.

'What do the boys wear?' I inquired.

'Why, they wear trousers, of course,' he smiled at me.

'Then I'll wear trousers too,' I told him.

'No, you will not,' he informed me, politely but firmly.

I was about to protest and tell him that I'd much rather be considered a boy, but caught my mother's stern look and decided to shut up.

Shiny and I were taken to a bright-green painted classroom for the entrance test. The room was full of fair-haired children, talking to each other in excited tones and unintelligible languages. There were also some Oriental faces. Later, I would learn to instantly differentiate between Chinese, Japanese, Korean, Thai and Filipino. But back then they all just looked the same. I mean, literally, the same – as if each one had exactly the same face. A striking black-haired girl caught my eye, because she looked Indian. She was speaking to a boy who also looked very Indian, but surprisingly they were speaking in a language I couldn't understand. They could be South Indian, I thought.

'Are you Indian?' I asked with a hopeful smile.

'No, we're South American,' the girl returned my smile. 'Hi, I'm Paola Solis,' she said and then proceeded to stretch out her hand. I was stunned. Whoever heard of a twelve-year-old offering a handshake? I complied feebly. She introduced the boy as Alisandro Lopez, but he didn't seem too keen to make my acquaintance. She was from Bolivia and he from Brazil. I had never known anyone from Bolivia, or Brazil, for that matter. In fact, I had never known anyone from anywhere other than India. Maybe I would even find Germans here.

The test was a breeze. Mr Jones was highly impressed and tried to hold a conversation with me, but I was more interested in listening to the language Paola and Alisandro conversed in. Blue Isle School was going to be a very fascinating place indeed.

On the first day of term, Shiny and I found ourselves in a large auditorium where the entire school had assembled. A kind-faced teacher directed us to where our respective classes should be.

'Is this 3W?' I asked a girl whose hair was strangely half-brown and half-gold. Even more shocking was the fact that she had lipstick on!

'Yes, but it's not 'three-dubbloo',' she mimicked me. 'It's three-double-you.'

I sensed she was being mean about something, but I couldn't put my finger on it, so I thanked her and sat down. My entire class looked so alien. They were all either white or Chinese, and looked so much more grown-up than me. To my utter horror I noticed that many of the girls wore make-up and jewellery. In Carmel Convent, they would have been skinned alive.

After the assembly, we trooped off to the 3W form-room. I sat on one of the front desks, feeling a little unsure and self-conscious for the first time in my life. There was total chaos all around me. Everyone was discussing that summer's football World Cup final – an ill-tempered match in which Germany had defeated Argentina. I listened to the banter absently, replaying in my mind the goals and fouls. A couple of boys were wrestling under the teacher's table. One girl was being dragged about by her hair, by a boy who sported even longer hair.

'Stop yanking my bra!' someone yelled. Shocked, I turned around, to see a very pretty girl telling off a boy.

'I was just checking if you're wearing one,' he told her with an elfin grin.

I couldn't believe my ears; I was sitting in a madhouse. And that's when I saw him. The noise seemed to just dissipate and everything else became a blur as he walked in. I was transfixed; I had actually never seen such Raphael-esque beauty. He looked like he'd just walked out of the Sistine Chapel, minus the wings.

A short while later, Mr Graham Stern, our Form Master, arrived and instead of the hush I would have expected, a roar erupted.

'Hi Mr Stern!'

'How were your holidays, Mr Stern?'

What kind of a school was this? Mr Stern then began to take attendance, and everyone answered his or her name with a 'Here!'

'. . . Jonathon Chambers, Zack Corrington, Stephen Courtney, . . . ' Names that seemed straight out of a book. I thought I saw the angel raise his hand for Zack Corrington.

'. . . Tanya Trivedi.'

Some pre-programmed mechanism in my body kicked into gear and I stood up on reflex and said, 'Present Sir!' The whole class erupted into laughter. Mr Stern scolded them and told me warmly that I needn't stand up when I answer attendance, or for asking any question. I felt very stupid and sat down. Mr Stern then asked a girl named Barkha Maithani to show me around and help me settle in.

'Since she's Indian, I think you might find it easier to talk to her in the beginning,' he said to me.

Barkha Maithani didn't look Indian in the least. Her coloured hair fell loose below her shoulders, wore a massive 'Peace' sign around her neck, and stood in fur-trimmed ankle-length boots.

'Hi Barkha,' I smiled at her.

'The name's Porsche,' she spat back. 'And I don't know why I'm the one who has to get stuck with you.'

'You don't have to,' I shot right back, despite being hurt. 'I can take care of myself.'

And that's how Blue Isle School began for me.

In the first week of classes, there was so much to learn, observe and absorb. For starters, they wore their shirts out, not tucked in. Everyone had different accents – British, Australian, South African, American and Irish. Sports period, to my delight, was an hour and twenty minutes daily, not one hour a week. I learnt that much like friendly neighbours India and Pakistan, there was no love lost between Australians and Kiwis. And I began to accept French-Thai or Japanese-Sri Lankan genetic hybrids as valid beings. Subconsciously through all this, I kept an eye on Zack.

The first time I noticed that I was noticing him was in Mrs Buskin's drama class. It was straight after lunch and everyone had assembled in class, except for him.

'Where's Zack?' I found myself wondering. And then I wondered why it mattered. Meanwhile, Mrs Buskin echoed my thoughts as she called out, 'Where's Zack? Why is he always late for my class?'

'Because your class is always after lunch, Mrs Buskin,' he walked in with a huge grin all over his face. He had been playing football and was dripping in sweat. I caught myself smiling for no apparent reason.

Mrs Buskin also taught us English and it was in my second English class that I first spoke to Zack Corrington. We had been given a text to read at home and were going to have a test based on that. I was sitting alone, as I often did for the first few weeks, and suddenly out of the blue Zack came and dumped his bag next to mine. I froze. I prayed that he wouldn't talk to me, because I wouldn't know what to say. He didn't attempt conversation at first, but halfway through the test, he suddenly whispered.

'What did you get for that?'

The words were garbled in my head. His eyes were like glowing amber. Then I swallowed something in my throat and said, 'What did I get for what?'

'Question four,' he said and looked into my paper without even asking me. He apparently found what he was looking for and began writing again.

My heart was in my mouth. As it is, I was extremely nervous because the academics there were too bizarre, and the test was unlike anything I had encountered before.

'What do you think Peterson should have done in that situation?' Question 7 asked.

What do I *think*? I don't know how to answer that. There was nothing about this in the text. What kind of a test was this? Was this a trick question?

After a few weeks, despite being from another galaxy, I began to settle in. Even Porsche became a friend, because I had given it to her as good as I had got. And I started acing all my classes, as I was used to doing back home. Doing well at academics or sport, or better still, both, won you friends and respect in any school, irrespective of your geographical location on the planet.

The sport part I figured out a few weeks later. The very first PE period I attended had very nearly been a disaster.

'What is your favourite sport?' the Bugs Bunny-like Miss Hughson asked, towering over me in her resplendent yellow T-shirt and white gym skirt, two buck-teeth glistening in the sun.

'I don't know,' I replied, trying hard to concentrate on what she was saying, because all I could hear was 'Err, what's up Doc?'

'You don't know?' she blinked at me as if I had spoken in Swahili,.

'Football or cricket I guess,' I said, shifting my weight, a little self-conscious. Miss Hughson fidgeted with the whistle that hung around her neck. How could anyone look so much like a cartoon?

'Well, we don't really have a cricket programme here and only the boys play football. Can you play netball?'

I hadn't even heard of that. Why couldn't I just play football, I implored. I was used to playing with boys back home in India; I could even perform the bicycle kick, I assured her. Reluctantly, Miss Hughson gave in and for my first semester at Island School I played football with the boys and learned what a huge gulf there was between the untaught, slapdash football we played in our Indian colonies and the skilled, precise and demanding football played in better schools around the world. I learnt free-throw strategies and how penalties are earned. I began to understand that an assist was nearly as important as the goal. It was like being on a new planet.

One sunny October afternoon Miss Hughson announced the start of the Cross Country season. Her comment was greeted with moans and groans of disapproval. I didn't protest because I didn't know what it was. Freckled and red-haired Emma Gough informed me that we were going to run five miles.

'Can you run?' Miss Hughson asked me, concerned. I thought she was daft. Admittedly, I had been a bit of a mess at netball and was a very poor swimmer, until then. But who didn't know how to run?

'Of course,' I replied indignantly. I was told to follow the crowd to remain on course. But Emma whispered to me that if I was a fast runner, I had better follow her because most of the others were 'slow oafs'. So I fastened my laces and began to follow her. We ran down the wooden steps, past the hillside garden and onto the road that wound its way up to the peak. I stayed with Emma and tried to make conversation, but she wouldn't speak and was breathing rhythmically, almost mechanically. Imitating her I continued running. A Chinese Pagoda garden was the halfway mark at which we had to touch the gate and then start running back. On the way back I found many students walking leisurely towards the pagoda, some had stopped moving altogether and were sitting and chatting or smoking. A sizeable number though, were still running. I was beginning to tire and started losing Emma but carried on running. A group of boys raced past me, including Zack Corrington. But before he went ahead he said something that didn't make sense.

'Good on you! You're doing well!'

Why was everyone acting as if I was disabled? I mean, what was the big deal in running? Eventually, I returned to the main football field. A dozen or so students were scattered about on the ground, drinking water and towelling off. Miss Hughson's eyes nearly popped out when she saw me.

'Did you run all the way?' she asked me sceptically. I was still panting. Emma Gough answered for me.

'Yes, she did. She ran with me most of the way.'

Miss Hughson gave me a huge thump on the back, with a big, toothy smile and said, 'Well done.' Zack Corrington came up and said, 'You're a good runner.'

'Am I?' I thought, genuinely unsure. After all, I had never participated in any organised sport. Back in India, sports had been entirely haphazard, substandard and unimportant. But clearly, I could run. Apparently I had not only been the second-fastest girl to go to Second Pagoda and back, but had also beaten ninety percent of the boys. Emma Gough happened to be the junior-girls' interschool champion. I soon was so fixated with cross-country running that the 5-mile run to Second Pagoda and back became the focal point of my existence. I trained at lunchtime and sometimes even after school. Whenever my friends and I were bored and short of ideas, I would eagerly suggest a good run. Needless to say, they all thought I was insane. But I made the school team that winter.

One afternoon, during a particularly tedious math class, Porsche asked me whom I had a crush on.

'What's a crush?' I asked her.

'You don't know what a crush is?' she stared at me, unbelieving. 'Are you from Mars?'

Alice Hui, a petite and pretty Chinese-American who sat next to me, explained the concept to me. I was outraged and insulted.

'What are you talking about?' I barked at both of them. 'I'm not interested in all that!'

Used to my ways by then, they both rolled their eyes and asked me a 'hypothetical' question.

'If you *were* interested, which guy would you have had a crush on?'

'Zack Corrington,' pat came out the reply, the speed of which startled even me.

'I thought so,' Porsche said and they both smiled.

Zack used to sit with Stephen, directly in front of us in math. The very next day, Stephen was absent and the seat next to Zack was free.

'Why don't you go sit next to him?' Alice suggested and Porsche giggled.

'Okay,' I said, thinking it was a great idea and to their absolute astonishment, I promptly picked up my books and plunked myself next to him. Alice and Porsche were in shock. Apparently people didn't behave like that. It was such a 'desperate' move they told me after class.

To me, it was just honest. And a move I never regretted. Because from that day onwards, began a fantastic friendship and a deeper, inexplicable bond that would last for years. Zack and I began to sit together in every class, passed notes, laughed, chatted on the phone for hours and discussed everything under the sun.

I learned to love English Premiership football, because he was apparently going to play for Liverpool someday. We discussed Ryan Giggs and Jamie Redknapp and the arrival of Pete Sampras and Monica Seles into the tennis world. I was also his shoulder to cry on. Once, he broke down after football because he had foiled a goal opportunity. All the other boys called him a loser, but I gave him a hug outside the boys' locker room and received a peck on my cheek in return.

I replayed the incident over and over in my head for the next few days and eventually decided it was best I go back to being a girl. Being a tomboy in a girls' convent awarded you rock-star status but in a co-ed school it branded you Boy George. Moreover, I realised that at Blue Isle I didn't need to be one of the boys to gain acceptance or love sport – one look at the pony-tailed, freckleface Emma Gough was enough to endorse that. And accordingly, my hair began to grow back out.

I was still in total denial about the crush, though. News travels fast, and Shiny heard about 'Tanya and Zack' in her class one day. Being far less bull-headed than me, Shiny had already become one of the crowd: having crushes, using foul language and wearing her school shirt pulled out instead of tucked in.

'Do you have a crush on Zack?' she asked me innocently one evening as we sat in our room doing our homework.

I gave her the lecture of a lifetime, telling her how corrupted she had become.

But it was blatantly obvious to everyone other than me, even to my teachers. In Art class, I would only draw boys that looked like Zack. In short-story writing, my lead character was always Zack. The thing that puzzled my friends was that I never felt jealous. Zack was incredibly popular with the ladies and had a different girlfriend practically every month, but it really, truly never bothered me. He would tell me all about his dates and necking sessions in graphic detail and although I would feel envious for a moment or two, I would also try to laugh and enjoy his accounts.

I even asked girls out for him when he didn't have the nerve. Like when he developed an interest in Paola Solis, but couldn't ask her out because he barely knew her. I promptly went ahead and asked her out for him. I really just wanted him to be happy. My friends couldn't understand it, and joked about the 'most unselfish love in the history of mankind'. Perhaps they were right.

Or perhaps there was so much else happening in my life that even at thirteen, I didn't have time for romance. One afternoon in early 1991, as we waited for Mr Stern to arrive for Form period,

Emma Gough introduced me to Wonderland. She announced loudly in class, 'Who wants to be a ball boy?'

'I do, I do!' shouted the green-eyed Allison Courtney, raising her hand as if a teacher had asked the question. A couple of boys also seemed interested. I was watching with detached amusement, unsure of what they were discussing when Emma turned to me.

'Aren't you interested?' she said as though it should be the most obvious thing in the world for me to want to be a ball boy. 'You love tennis, don't you?'

It dawned upon me like the enlightenment of the Buddha. Of course I knew what ball boys were! Steffi Graf never forgot to thank them in any of her victory speeches. I suddenly felt an unparalleled rush of excitement. Could I actually be one of those privileged creatures who walked on the same courts as the tennis gods?

'Of course I do!' I leaped out of my seat in enthusiasm. 'What do I have to do to become a ball boy?'

Not much, apparently, if you went to one of the four, elite British schools in Hong Kong. All I did that following weekend was participate in a couple of hours of running between baselines and catching and throwing tennis balls, and at the end of the session held at the Victoria Park Sports Centre, I was officially recruited into the Hong Kong Tennis Association as a 'ball person'. It was the best thing that had ever happened to me.

First, and this was a pleasant surprise – it made me rich. I would have gladly done it for free, but to my delight found that ball boys were paid a handsome 100 Hong Kong dollars a day during tournaments. I'd have 700 dollars in my pocket at the end of the week and could more than just afford to go out with all my pocket-money-loaded friends for movies and lunches from then on.

No more 'Honestly, the five-dollar meal combo is really my favourite.'

Second, top-rung ATP tournaments became my own private utopia to which I would escape a few times a year. The routine tribulations of teenage, like unrequited crushes and image crises, meant little to me. I was absorbed in my world, where the tennis gods ruled. And I got to meet nearly all of them. Tournament after tournament, I laboured happily on the courts, rewarded by the chance to observe the speed of a Richard Krajicek serve from an arm's length, or to witness in-person the historic moment Pete Sampras first became No.1 in the world.

It was a dream come true to be able to occasionally even indulge in banter with my idols. But it didn't always go well, like when Ivan Groucho Lendl yelled at me on national television. He was struggling to hold serve and apparently I had not fed him the ball straight enough. Indeed I had not, because I had been too absorbed with Stefan Edberg's legs across the court.

I did better with Wimbledon champion Michael Stich though. Zack Corrington was half German, so I thought I'd kill two birds with one stone – learn a phrase in Deutsch and make Zack jealous at the same time. He promised to teach me a real eyebrow-raiser, but only if I would trust him and not ask him what it meant. I reluctantly agreed to the gamble.

'*Haben Sie ein Kaninchen, Michael?*' I said to Michael Stich that evening, yelling for my voice to be heard over a din of autograph-seeking ball boys.

To my amazement, it worked like a dream. Busily signing autographs and posing for the odd photo, Stich startled, looked straight down at me and exploded into laughter. What had I said? Then he said something in German, but noting my clueless expression, switched to English.

'Why do you want to know that?' he chuckled, shaking his head as though he couldn't quite believe what I had asked him. He was talking to me! I was thrilled but wondered whether I had said something really embarrassing.

'I don't even know what I said,' I confided, feeling extremely silly suddenly but thrilled to bits nonetheless. 'A German friend told me to say that. What did I say?'

This set him off again. 'You just asked me if I have a rabbit,' he guffawed even as he looked at the rest of the ball girls who had formed an envious audience by now. I was mortified and wanted to kill Zach. What a stupid question! But then, Stich chortled some more and said fondly, 'Come here, let's take a picture with you.' And that photograph with a huge, stupid grin plastered across my face and the reigning Wimbledon champion's arm around my shoulders held the pride of being on my mantelpiece for years.

Dreams of winning Wimbledon myself someday egged me onto charting my life's course around three things: tennis, sports, and fitness. I even controlled my diet like a professional athlete, read up on training programmes and whatever else I could get my hands on. Nothing else mattered, not even Zack.

Because the real romances went on in my head. I went out on a date with Stefan Edberg at the Stockholm Masters and performed Wicca spells to materialise Stich in my bedroom. I enjoyed a romantic dinner in Monte Carlo with Goran Ivanisevic and of course, lived happily ever after with Boris Becker at the end of every fantasy. I did occasionally go out on dates from school, but to me the real men were the tennis pros, the guys I handed the towels to on court. I felt giddy when Pete Sampras spent five minutes talking to me or Jim Courier handed me an appreciative Ferrero Rocher. That was the real deal. The boys at school just didn't compare.

Eight

The Camp of Sin

The rumour doing the rounds was that the prefects were having a party. We weren't presumptuous enough to think we'd be invited but we wanted to have one of our own. Unfortunately no one thought a single-sex party was any fun. An hour after the barbecue, we were reluctantly herded into our respective dormitories. Vicky Lester, the prefect who made all the boys drool, actually locked us in. Like cattle. They certainly didn't want us to see whatever they were going to get up to.

We were in Lantau – Hong Kong's version of paradise island. Of the about 230 islands officially belonging to the territory of Hong Kong, Lantau is the largest, bigger than even Hong Kong itself. And it's virtually untouched. At least it was back then.

A hundred and eighty four teen-year-olds were in Lantau for a week. Every academic year there would be one week of camping, and an entire batch of students would disappear off into the hills, islands or rural mainland territories surrounding Hong Kong.

All six sections of Third and Fourth Form – Da Vinci, Einstein, Fleming, Nansen, Rutherford and Wilberforce – had braved an eventful two-hour steamboat ride from Hong Kong to Lantau Island. We were all very excited, me most of all, because until then my only exposure to camping had been storybooks. With great fanfare we had boarded the steamer, and looked out into the open ocean from the wide deck. There was cake and biscuits and iced tea by the gallon, and as adolescents are wont to do, we stuffed ourselves silly, singing, chattering and laughing all the while.

And then someone mentioned the word seasickness. It first came from the far side of the deck, where the Einstein bunch was standing. A girl with a long, blond ponytail was doubled up over the railing, presumably throwing up.

'Seasickness . . . ' the whispers started.

Until then, no one had noticed the steamer's movement, but suddenly all of us felt each wave hit like a tsunami. Panic spreads fast, and the epidemic had already struck. Within minutes, everyone knew just how much everyone else had had for lunch. The food certainly wasn't to blame – the teachers and prefects had nibbled on the same refreshments and they felt perfectly fine. Only the younger lot were affected, which would have been quite acceptable, except that about a hundred and twenty of us were being sick simultaneously. The self-assured teachers and prefects were suddenly at a total loss for what to do, as more of us succumbed to the contagion.

Only one teacher went about diligently mopping up, picking up students and planting them on the chairs inside, in the shaded cabin. Like a messiah, he handed out cups of cold water and comforted those who had nearly passed out. He was the Honourable Mister John Temp, our religious education teacher.

We all loved him, even before his healing touch aboard the Lantau-bound steamer. The subject he taught did not exactly give Sex Education a run for its money on the popularity charts, but Mr Temp was always warm, gentle and so terribly earnest. We never had the heart to let on that we were not quite as pious as him, and yawns were always respectfully stifled in his class. Of course, there was the odd religious education class that inspired interest. Like the one on Hindu mythology, where everyone was so stunned to learn that a particular Hindu god had an elephant's head that they all turned to look at me in wonder as though I had one too.

'He's going to be my favourite god from now on,' Emma Gough had whispered to me after that. 'I think he's so cool.'

And so, because of the godsend called Mr Temp, we did survive that trip to Lantau and arrived at Silvermine Bay, where the century-old Po Lin monastery beckoned. The monastery was breathtakingly beautiful — lush vegetation, fishponds, and fountains and hills rising majestically in the background. On the highest peak was a grand copper statue of the Tian Tian Buddha, so gigantic that it was clearly visible from miles out at sea. It is said to weigh 250 tons — the biggest Buddha statue in Asia.

First on the agenda was the camp itself, a short bus-ride away from Po Lin. And that was a legend in itself. The corridors were clean, but in a state of disrepair, some of the windowpanes were broken and the beds were flimsy iron cots befitting a prison cell. There were shrieks of dismay all around me. I tried to put on an aptly disgusted expression and blend in, but in reality I wasn't all that appalled. It was nothing I had not seen before in India, but that of course I couldn't broadcast. So I frowned harder and made some more disgruntled noises.

The best was yet to come though. Most of us were desperate for the bathroom and when there was a mass movement in that direction, nobody was prepared for the sight that followed.

'There are no toilets!' Allison Courtney came out screaming, her emerald eyes wide. 'There are just holes in the ground!'

Gasps and exclamations of disbelief were followed by many personal inspections, all with the same result. I had a sneaky feeling that I wasn't going to find it all that unfamiliar. Cautiously I ventured up to one cubicle, fervently hoping that it would be some grotesque, archaic arrangement and not what we call the good old 'Indian toilet'.

But the good old Indian toilet it was.

'And there's no toilet paper either!' Someone wailed. I think a couple of the girls were actually sniffling. 'What are we going to do?'

'Maybe the Chinese drip dry,' some Smart Alec noted.

There were more shocks in store, foremost among them the fact that the boys and girls would be staying far apart. Separate dormitories were understood, but what no one was prepared for was that the boy's quarters were more than a kilometre up the hill.

Great moans of disappointment, predominantly emanating from the girls. We were of the age when girls are interested solely in boys and nothing else. The boys were struggling with hormones too, but sport was their No.1 interest and they weren't old enough to start thinking of girls as sport, just yet. I was an anomaly because I was as interested in sport as I was in boys.

Dinner consisted of fried rice with frog meat, and the next day it was '*choi sam*' with garden snake. At first I thought the man at the canteen was pulling a fast one on us, but when I noticed my classmates accept the frog meat quite solemnly, I speechlessly took my tray. And then everyone began to eat with chopsticks. I was stunned – all these Caucasian kids chomping away happily with chopsticks! Didn't you need special DNA to do that? I was definitely going to need something special, but for the first day I settled on my reliable Indian hand, as there was nothing else available. Decorum be damned. The next day Jonathon Chambers taught me how to use chopsticks and I was surprised at how quickly I caught on. It wasn't genetics after all.

Our days were packed tight with organised activities like canoeing, basketball, rock-climbing or trekking, observed by the hawk-eyed Sixth Form prefects. There were also nature workshops, geography classes and Orientation – essentially an exercise in map reading. Mr Temp would then take an afternoon class on Buddhism and East Asian philosophy.

But the evenings were free for us to do whatever we wanted. One Wednesday evening, a small group of us was strolling along Mui Wo Chung Hau Street and we sauntered into a nearby village market. There was a small stall that rented out bicycles. I was thrilled. I was as familiar with rented bicycles as my peers were with rock climbing. I suggested that we all take one and go 'explore' the countryside. None of the girls seemed interested other than Porsche, and some of them even admitted to not knowing how to ride one. I immediately decided to be a hero and impress everyone, particularly Zack Corrington.

Picking up from where I had left off at the government colony back in India, I pompously asked the stall owner for an adult-sized men's cycle, much to his astonishment.

'Can you really ride that?' Zack asked me, his hazel eyes shining with sheer respect.

'Of course,' I said with a nonchalant shrug of the shoulder and proceeded to step onto a low stone bench, and then atop the cycle. Coolly I rode off, whistling for effect.

I had not counted on two things.

One, it had been almost eighteen months since I last rode a cycle.

Two, cycling on sand was something else altogether.

Less than five metres away from my friends, I came crashing back down to earth. I was so embarrassed I wanted to dig myself into the sand. Zack came running to my side.

'Are you hurt?' he said, concerned and lifted the enormous cycle off me. I shrugged and tried to stand up.

'I don't believe this!' I wailed. 'I really can ride a bike that size,' I tried to explain to everyone so they wouldn't think of me as asinine and boastful. But it only made me sound more idiotic.

Zack helped me limp back to the camp, where I got first aid for a pretty nasty gash on my knee and then we were off on the bikes once again. This time though, I chose one with more appropriate dimensions.

That was the night the prefects decided to have some fun. The teachers were invited of course. We couldn't care less about the stupid party. We had enough problems of our own to contend with, the epicentre of which was being locked in the dorm. Michelle Porter was in distress because she couldn't be with her latest boyfriend, Tim Howells. Alice Hui was wrapped around a pillow, theatrically announcing that it was a substitute for Justin Mueller. The stunning, auburn-haired Vera Locke was dying to see what the boys looked like in their pyjamas. Everyone was miserable. By the time the complaints had turned into a cacophony of moans and groans, I just couldn't stand it any longer.

'Oh God! Stop it all of you,' I snapped, generating sudden silence. 'If we can't have any fun without them, then let's go join them!'

'How,' wailed Michelle. 'That stupid cow Vicky locked us in.'

Melissa Lowness with the half-gold, half-brown hair had been sitting quietly on her bunk, painting her nails red all this while and looking bored. 'You know, if you're all so desperate, just jump out the bloody window,' she said in her clipped Latin American accent. 'What's the big deal?'

'You know she's right!' I exclaimed. 'The windows are open, you morons. We can all just go!'

Utter excitement. Everyone was scrambling up onto the windowsill to see how far we would have to jump. The windows were pretty high in the double-vaulted dormitory, but the fall couldn't have been more than about eight feet. It looked quite entirely possible. The only problem that I saw was that I saw nothing. It was pitch black outside, not a single lamp anywhere on the vast darkness of hillside that stretched behind the building. The boys' dorms were somewhere up that hill.

'Okay, who wants to go?' I asked, turning around, perched atop the windowsill. There were a few unsure murmurs and a few emphatic affirmatives.

'You guys are crazy,' said the hoity-toity Avery Merchant, her wire-rimmed glasses perched over her hooked Parsi nose. 'Do you have any clue how much trouble you'll get into?'

There were many who agreed with her and in the end only about fifteen of us had mustered up the nerve. Or were as desperate, if you subscribed to Melissa's theory. But Mel herself wasn't quite so dour. Despite her sarcastic comment, which had initiated the revolution, she was game for the adventure. Tuck was packed into a bed-sheet, torches were switched on and one by one, we started jumping off the window and out into freedom.

I led at the front with the most powerful torch in my hand, while Mel guarded the back end of the queue. The delicate darlings were sandwiched in the middle. Step by step we inched our way up the hill. Slipping, sliding, wavering torch beams guiding the way. Thankfully, no one saw us but should they have, what a sight we would have been – a single file of thirteen-year-old girls clothed in an assortment of nighties and pyjamas, scrambling up a hill on all fours, in the dead of the night and in the middle of nowhere.

Today I wonder if I'd have the courage. Or for that matter, be as desperate.

By a miracle of fortune we actually found the boys' dorms. They were clearly fast asleep as the lights were out and there wasn't a sound emanating from inside. Evidently, they hadn't been pining for us the way we had been. What a pity.

Melissa decided to get on with it and pounded on the door. A medley of noises erupted. Amid shrieks, questions, bellows and confusion, rugby hero Victor Rose opened the door. In boxers. Vera gasped.

'Hi Vicks,' we sang in chorus even as he rubbed his eyes, literally. And then he broke out into his trademark fanged smile.

'By Joe! What a surprise,' he grinned, totally oblivious of his semi-clad state. 'C'mon in, girls!'

The midnight procession marched into the room as lights were switched on, quilts were quickly grabbed, and exclamations of all sorts rang around the hall. Not all the boys were pleased with the unexpected arrivals. Especially the ones who preferred to sleep in the buff. Allison Courtney's twin, Stephen, for example, flung his shoes at us. But he was heavily outnumbered.

'Am I dreaming or has God answered my prayers?' Chris Cuthbert jested from his overhead bunk.

I was scanning the room for Zack and just as I spotted him, he smiled at me, perched atop a bunk a few beds away.

'I hope you brought Celina along,' he shouted out with a hopeful grin. Just wonderful. I was not going to ruin my midnight party playing audience to Zack and his love sagas.

'You know this is not her kind of "thing",' I said of the high-and-mighty Miss Celina Kay Ross, his latest love interest, as I walked up to him and he nodded in resigned comprehension. He swung himself off his bed and we joined the large group in the centre even as a few of the boys went to call others from the adjacent dorms. We ate, played Spin The Bottle and Truth Or Dare halfway into the night. A few couples sank into dark corners and got up to their usual business, while the rest of us who weren't quite so lucky made up for it with obscene jokes.

When it was almost one in the morning, most of the girls got up to leave. But I was having too much fun. And so were Vera, Melissa, Emma, Alice and Sonia Sheikh, apparently. The six of us decided to stay on and play a few more rounds of Truth Or Dare. Every now and then Chris would make us jump out of our skins by announcing that he saw some teacher or the other outside the window. To punish him we gave him a particularly difficult dare when it was his turn. He had to stuff his vest with tissue to look a bit like Juliet, and then step out and cry, 'Romeo, Romeo, wherefore art thou Romeo?' to the quiet stillness outside. He accepted the challenge with gusto.

But no sooner had he stepped out than he came back running, yelling, 'Mr Temp's here! Mr Temp's coming!'

We all rolled our eyes and cursed him for trying yet another stupid stunt. But he didn't stop.

'I'm serious, he's right here!' He yelled, his face white. 'Get out of here!'

By the time it dawned upon us that he might be telling the truth, it was almost too late. We could actually hear the footsteps outside.

'Quick!' Mel yelled. 'Get under the beds.'

In a flash, all six of us darted under one bed each, even as somebody switched off the lights. Just as Mr Temp swung the door open, each and every boy had dived back into bed, not necessarily his own.

Pin-drop silence as Mr Temp's buffed shoes slowly came into view, moonlight shining in from the outside.

'You boys are still awake?' he asked slowly, and I held my breath. 'I saw the lights on just a few seconds ago. C'mon boys, own up! I want to know who switched off the lights.'

Not a sound. No reply from the boys. And certainly not from the girls. Somebody pretended to snore. Quite rightly assuming that no one was going to 'own up', Mr Temp walked across to the switches and the room flooded with light. My heart jumped. Thankfully, we were not in Mr Temp's field of vision.

'What's going on, Rob? Daniel?' he asked the boys on the nearest bed. 'Why are you both on the same bed?' I had to stifle a giggle. Vera winked at me from under their bed.

'Nothing, Mr Temp, we were chatting, that's all,' Rob said with a very straight face.

'Allright then, it's not like I'm going to get angry. I just want to know who switched off the lights just now.'

That got the boys breathing again and a lot of voices started talking to Mr Temp at the same time. He really didn't seem angry at all. Under the bed directly opposite me, I could see Emma smothering herself to keep from laughing. We were going to get away with it after all.

'*What's that!*' Mr Temp's baritone reverberated suddenly and we all froze again. I saw his shoes coming down the dorm, in our direction. The shoes stopped short, just two beds away from me. Then I saw hands come down and pick something up; it looked like some kind of rope emanating from under the bed sheet. His hand pulled back up, and with it came up the head that was attached to the rope. Sonia Sheikh's waist-length permed hair had given her away!

As Sonia would later tell us, Mr Temp looked like his eyes were going to pop out of his head.

'Sonia Sheikh! *What are you doing here?*' We had never heard Mr Temp shout ever before. But at that moment, he wasn't just shouting, he was bellowing with rage. 'This is shameful, shameful! What would your parents think should I tell them I found you in the boys' dorm at two in the morning?'

'I'm not the only one,' she replied meekly, a tone entirely unbecoming of her sharp American twang. After a few seconds of silence, Mr Temp said in a somewhat more controlled voice, 'What do you mean?'

Before Sonia could answer, Mel did a most admirable thing and slipped out from under Chris' bed. Chris sat there looking highly uncomfortable, with the tissues still rendering a 34B bust.

'She means there are more of us here and it's no big deal,' Mel said, looking Mr Temp straight in the eye. That was our cue. One by one, each one of us crept out from under the beds and stood in a straight line in front of Mr Temp. Mel, Emma and Alice looked very defiant, but I was mortified. Mr Temp was speechless. Eventually he found his tongue.

'I am so shocked and disappointed that despite everything that I have taught you, you girls have behaved in this disgraceful manner. Shame on you.'

Mel began to giggle and I was truly horrified. It was one thing to have some sneaky fun, but something else altogether to totally disrespect a teacher.

'I'm too angry to even think right now,' he said, his lips actually quivering in fury. All the boys were silent spectators by now. 'Get back to your dorms right now.'

When he said 'tomorrow morning I will inform your parents and then hand out an appropriate punishment,' I instantly wished he would hand out capital punishment. Anything would be better than facing the wrath of my intensely moralistic Indian mother in her Kali avatar. Silently we trooped back down the hill, in exactly the opposite mood to the one we had come up in.

I lay awake half the night, dreading the consequences. But the call was never made. In fact, the next morning Mr Temp was a changed man, more like the Mr Temp we all knew and loved. He wasn't quite so furious anymore, but of course, we still had to be punished. The five offenders were made to wash the dishes of the entire camp, after breakfast. Our sinful deeds were declared to everyone and once the tables were cleared, we got working on the dirty plates – all hundred and eighty of them. If you count the teachers and the prefects, it was a good two hundred. Mel and

Alice felt humiliated, but the rest of us didn't mind in the least bit. In fact, as she was handing her plate to us, Rutherford Form Master Ms Pierre even winked at us as if to say 'hope you had a good time while you were at it'.

Later that day we found out just why Mr Temp had been in so black a mood the night before. Apparently, a couple of tipsy prefects had stumbled onto Mr Chan and Miss Hammond in the latter's room and well, the two had not exactly been playing scrabble. Teachers were simply not supposed to get caught indulging in amorous activities, and certainly not by students. In fact, in Mr Temp's book, teachers were probably not supposed to be up to such activities in the first place. So, Mr Temp had stormed out of the party and gone to check on the boys instead. Only to walk into us. No wonder the poor devout man lost his head. And I bet he still remembers the Camp of Sin to this day and shakes his head in dismay the way only Mr Temp can.

Nine

Runaways

I rang the buzzer from outside the building's main lobby, my fingers trembling with foreboding, and perhaps, the cold. Popi, the maid, came on the intercom and whispered hoarsely, 'Tanya, is that you?'

It was quarter to three in the morning, I had stolen out of the house without permission, had journeyed all the way to mainland China and back, escorted by the police for part of the expedition. And now, I was facing certain annihilation. If nothing else, my parents would deport me to India the very next day, I was sure of that. All that had transpired in the last two weeks rushed before my eyes, even as Popi pressed the buzzer to let me in.

The unfortunate trouble began with a new golf-and-tennis facility called Mission Hills in Shenzhen, China, which was being thrown open to the world in a couple of weeks' time. A grand ceremony had been planned, and sports personalities, pop stars and world celebrities were invited. The utmost source of excitement for my immediate circle of friends, who under normal circumstances would have zilch interest in anything sporting, was the fact that an American pop singer called Tommy Rage was to perform for the gala opening. Barring me, they were all rabid music fans. No self-respecting fourteen-year-old would be caught dead without their earphones. I clearly had no pride because I didn't even own a Discman. I was also the lone one who harboured no affection for the deplorable Tommy Rage, who sang only mushy, nauseating love ballads.

'How can he have the audacity to do so when he's so ugly?' I would implore, referring to his colossal, blubbery nose. Nope, he just didn't meet my standards.

But then Tommy Rage decided to come to China in December of 1992. Back then, Hong Kong was still a British colony, so Shenzhen was actually another country. Not that it deterred my comrades in any way. The plans were made almost instantly. We had to go to the concert they said; there was simply no question about it.

'Are you kidding me?' I laughed. 'There's no way I'm going to a Tommy Rage concert. I'll probably puke and die.'

Moreover, the Barcelona Olympics were on and I was preoccupied with watching every minute of the live telecast. It was an unbelievably exciting edition of the Games, with men's basketball being thrown open to professionals, and the United States sending a 'Dream Team' that included Magic Johnson, Michael Jordan and Larry Bird. It was all too good to miss even a single night.

But then suddenly the words 'Exhibition Match between Steffi Graf and Arantxa Sanchez-Vicario' leapt out at me from the publicity poster that Vera was waving under my nose. Now *this* changed the situation entirely. Hong Kong hosted several top ATP tournaments round the year, but none for women, or the WTA events to be precise. And despite working for the HKTA for almost two years, I had never laid eyes on my ultimate idol and inspiration – Steffi Graf. An opportunity to watch her in flesh was not to be passed up. Instantly, I was game and suggested we include my Korean friend Sang-Kee in the mission, as she too was a hardcore fan. Of Tommy Rage, not Steffi Graf, of course.

Parental permissions came fast and easy for most of the others. In my case I came upon a brick wall.

'Are you mad?' was my father's first response, several weeks before the concert. 'Do you know where Shenzhen is? Do you know it's in China?'

'I know that,' I insolently shouted back. 'So what's the big deal? There are trains that run to and fro, Vera has already found out. We'll be back in a few hours! Everyone else's parents have given them permission. Why must you both always be spoil-sports?'

'All your friends hold Hong Kong passports,' Papa tried to reason with me. 'They won't have to go through immigration.'

'Sang-Kee doesn't. She's Korean.'

'I don't care if she's Korean, she's not my daughter.'

'How can you be so mean, Papa?' I wailed. 'All my friends will be going. And I love Steffi!' I tried to add an emotional angle to the plea.

'That's irrelevant. You're just a kid; you can't go to China on your own. And that's final.'

The conversation was over. Why do adults think they have the right to make life-altering decisions on others' behalf without so much as an explanation? It was infuriating to be fourteen and powerless. Despondent, I informed my friends that I would not be meeting Steffi Graf after all, or Tommy Rage for that matter. Sang-Kee too had been denied permission for much the same reasons after all. With less than a week to go for the event, I turned desperate and finally tried Barkha 'Porsche' Maithani's original suggestion of plain old lies. Over dinner, I informed my parents that Vera was having a party the coming Friday.

'Isn't Friday, the 7th?' Papa asked casually.

'Yes,' I replied, hoping he would have forgotten all mention of Tommy Rage by now.

'Do you think I'm a fool?' Papa snapped. '7th is that Mission Valley or something event. You're not going to any party or any concert. This discussion was over long ago.'

So much for trying to hoodwink my father. With tears streaming down my cheeks, I choked on my dinner. I could see no light at the end of the tunnel.

And then came the greatest twist of fate. With just two days to go, I overheard a conversation between my parents that suggested they were going out for dinner on the 7th. Not wanting to raise any suspicions, I interrogated Popi, who was always in on their plans.

'Are they going out on Friday night?' I asked her, hope blossoming in my heart.

'Yes, they are,' she said, eyeing me warily. 'They have a diplomatic dinner to attend.'

'Where is it?' I almost jumped on her.

And she said the magic words: 'Macaaauuuuuuu.' Ka-Ching! I could hear the Jackpot. Macau was the playground of the Hong Kong's rich – the gambling capital of Asia. And more importantly, it was a good one-hour's boat ride away from Hong Kong. I quickly did the math in my head. With the minimum three hours they would spend hobnobbing at the do, they should be gone for well over six hours! I couldn't believe my luck. It might just be possible. Excitedly, I called Vera and the new plan began to formulate.

Friday evening arrived after what seemed like an eternity. I could barely concentrate on my tennis lesson that evening, struggling to focus on the slice serve that my coach was trying to add to my repertoire. Light was fading by the time I rushed home to find Papa waiting in the living room, talking to Shiny, while Mum was getting dressed. Popi was informed what she was to feed us for dinner. Tension filled the air.

It was almost six-thirty when my parents finally stepped out, the scent of Dior'ismo lingering on after Mum had shut the door behind her. Instantly, all hell broke loose and everything went into fast-forward mode. Clothes went flying out of my cupboard – the white T-shirt, black miniskirt and black waistcoat that were the decided 'dress code' for the day. Shiny handed out the lipstick while Popi fetched my calf-length boots. In about six minutes flat, I was ready and racing to the elevator. If I didn't meet my friends by seven, they would assume I hadn't been able to make it, and leave. I was literally praying under my breath.

Minibus No. 28 touched down at the Mass Transit Railway station at Queensway Central at a few minutes past seven-thirty, and my pulse was racing. Dashing down the stairs, I scanned the crowds for familiar faces. I couldn't have missed them if I tried – five girls dressed in identical fashion, holding aloft posters of the aforementioned Mr Rage. I rushed forward to greet Vera, Porsche, Alice, Avery and Sonia. Vera looked like a supermodel dressed for an acting role and Sonia made even the unadventurous waistcoat-and-shirt ensemble look like rocker chic, if that were somehow possible.

Thankfully, they had already bought my ticket. Vera hollered commands and we ran further down to the platform. The next quarter of an hour went by in a blur. We took the MTR to Tsim Sha Tsui, crossing over into the Kowloon side of Hong Kong, adjoining mainland China. From there we were to board the Kowloon Canton Railway's 19:30 train to Huanggang. Vera and Porsche had meticulously planned everything; the rest of us simply scurried behind them blindly.

Suddenly, looming large ahead of me was a cubicle marked 'Passport Check'. Feeling a bit unsure, I reached into my purse for my passport. But Vera, as always, had a better plan.

'Just keep running,' she whispered to all of us in general and me, in particular. 'Guys, surround Tanya. Three at the front, two behind.'

Everyone adhered to her instructions and they herded me along to the Hong Kong Nationals queue. There were just a few people in line. Apparently no one else thought the Mission Hills opening was a be-there-or-be-square event. Vera and Porsche startled me by kicking up a ruckus – shouting in Cantonese at the officer who stood at passport control. I was almost inconspicuous in the middle of the flock. Comprehension dawned upon the officer and his face lit up into an indulgent smile.

'Tommy Rage, ah? Mission Hills, ah?' he grinned at Vera, pointing at the ticket. She replied with a smile and an animated nod of the head. Sonia pointed to her watch furiously, telling him we would miss the train if he held us up any longer. He took a cursory glance at all the passports that were being waved in his face and then, in a moment of sheer commotion, let us through. We made a mad dash for the train and boarded, literally, as the doors pressed shut.

A collective sigh of relief. And hugs all around. And shrieks of joy. I had to sit down and calm myself. So much for my father's apprehensions of my not being a Hong Kong national. Out of the blue, I found it hilarious and burst out laughing. That set the others off and soon we were hysterical, rolling on the stainless steel seats of the train. There were a few other people on board, mostly wrinkly old locals, and they gave us dirty looks. That only made us laugh harder. We eventually settled down for the almost one-and-a-half-hour ride, six 14-year-olds dressed like waitresses, giddy with excitement.

From Huanggang, the Mission Hills Club resort complex was another half-hour road-trip away. There were two stations, east and west, but we couldn't figure out which one we were supposed to get off at, so we just hopped off at the first one arbitrarily. It was ten minutes short of nine o'clock and there was not a soul in sight. Our voices echoed even if we whispered. There were enough signboards for directions, but unfortunately, they were all in Cantonese. None of my friends could read the language, even though most of them could speak it quite fluently, except for Alice and Avery. We came upon a stairway leading upward, and climbed out into the open. Once again, not a person around. It was dark by now and there was no lighting whatsoever.

'Whatever happened to the streetlights?' questioned Sonia, tugging at her long curls as always.

'Everything's not Hong Kong,' I spoke to her silhouette. 'There are cities in the world where street lamps are dysfunctional. Trust me, I grew up in one.'

The others were meanwhile, scratching their heads.

'How come there's no sign of the Mission Hills event?' Porsche asked. 'Do you think we've come through the wrong exit?'

'Do you think we've come to the wrong *city*?' Avery muttered, adjusting her glasses and then lighting up a cigarette. She was the only one among my friends who smoked, although I had sneaked a puff on occasion.

'Vera, this is Shenzhen, isn't it?' I questioned, suddenly very worried.

'Of course this is Shenzhen! What's wrong with you guys? I'm not retarded. Maybe we should have exited from the West station.'

A short way down the street, we saw a car's headlights. And then another's. They were moving towards us, and before we knew it, the driver pulled over, poked his head out and said, 'Taxi?'

Oh yes, you bet! Immediately Vera showed him the concert tickets and as he nodded in comprehension, we started filing into the two cabs. Vera, Porsche and Sonia got into the first one, and Avery, Alice and I sat in the one that followed. We were almost there!

The driver strained his neck to look at us, blinking expectantly, and said something that was as comprehensible to us as Greek.

The three of us just blinked back.

He repeated it, and this time he sounded irritated.

'What's he saying?' I asked. No one said anything for a few seconds.

'In case you didn't know, I don't speak Chinese,' Avery said sarcastically. And we both turned to look at Alice. She too, shook her head.

'Fantastic!' exclaimed Avery. 'The entire Cantonese-speaking bunch has gone off in one cab. What's wrong with you,' Avery said turning to Alice. 'You're half Chinese! Why the hell don't you speak Chinese?'

'What's wrong with you, I should ask,' Alice spat back, her eyes narrowing even further. 'I have lived in New York all my life, while you were born and brought up here. Why on earth don't *you* speak Cantonese?'

'Oh stop it both of you,' I had to shush them up like a school teacher.

We proceeded to try and explain the destination to the cab driver, showing him the tickets, and making a few incomprehensible sounds – our feeble attempt at Cantonese. We had already lost the other cab, and let's not forget – this was the era before cell phones. But our driver nodded his head, got into gear and took off. We could only hope he had got the right message. It turned out to be another long ride, and several times along the way we felt distinctly uneasy. Avery was quick to paint the worst possible scenarios and we all breathed a sigh of relief when a huge entrance edifice came into view, just a few minutes before half-past nine. It was the Mission Hills Opening Ceremony all right – lights beamed high into the sky, music blared and the street was littered with fliers, all printed in Chinese. This was it; we'd made it. We paid the fare in Hong Kong dollars, much to the delight of the cabbie, and dashed off towards the nearest entry point.

Apparently, it wasn't the one printed on our ticket. The guard pointed at our tickets and gestured towards the left. We set off again, running around the perimeter of the tennis stadium. The fact that we could hear Tommy Rage singing only made it worse for Avery and Alice – they couldn't bear the thought of being so near and yet so far. It wasn't the next gate either, but we were so desperate to barge in that to Avery's horror, Alice and I actually got down on our knees and begged to be let in. Pantomime is evidently the universal language – the guard grunted approval and let us through.

At last, we had arrived upon our destination and the euphoria we felt in there, on the stands, was unmatched. We had made it just in time to catch the crescendo of the musical concert. Tommy Rage was about halfway through his performance and that meant he was crooning his top chartbusters. Thousands of people, mostly teenagers, swayed in unison as he delved into 'I'll be . . . your anything.' I had to admit, the atmosphere, the fireworks and the live music actually made Tommy Rage sound tolerable! Avery was nearly moved to tears, Alice was transfixed, and I was just soaking it all up.

Soon it was time for the musical extravaganza to take a break and the exhibition match to commence. Now starts the real action, I thought to myself, shivering with anticipation.

'There she is!' I exclaimed as a gazelle of a woman stepped onto the court with gentle, languid grace, waving and smiling at the crowds, a halo of light emanating from her golden head. Steffi Graf was beautiful. What I wouldn't have done to be a ball girl on that court!

'She looks like a goddess,' I whispered, mesmerised. Alice and Avery only giggled. Arantxa Sanchez-Vicario skipped in behind her, full of childlike energy.

Even as we enjoyed a rare genial match between the old foes, our eyes kept scanning the crowds to look for the other half of our gang. But it was pointless – much as we tried, it simply wasn't possible to locate three faces among teeming millions. At half past ten, the single-set match was over all too soon, 6-2 to Graf, no surprises there. Before I knew it, Steffi had disappeared into the cavernous black of the players' entrance and it was time for one of the musical acts again. I couldn't help feel a twinge of disappointment.

'What should we do about the others?' I wondered aloud, still giddy from watching Steffi in action. That forehand was twice as intimidating in real life. Was it possible for me to be in love with someone of the same sex, I thought, even as Canto pop-star Aaron Kwok came on and launched into *'Ngoi Nay'* or 'Love You'.

'We have to find them,' Avery stated matter-of-factly. 'How will we get back if we don't?'

'Do you think we should ask one of the security guards for help?' Alice said.

'Oh yeah, and if they don't speak English, let's just try French,' Avery snapped.

'What's wrong with you?' I retorted. 'Why are you behaving like this?'

'I'm sorry,' she said, losing the scornfulness entirely and I realised she was on the verge of tears again. 'I'm terrified we'll never find our way back to Hong Kong.'

The three of us walked up to the nearest security guard who was patrolling our stand. We tried to explain our situation to him, in vain of course. Alice then bravely decided to put her extremely deficient Cantonese to the test. And she said something, which loosely translated in to 'Three . . . girls . . . clothes . . . same.' It took a few repeated attempts and much gesticulation from Avery, and me in the background, but he eventually seemed to get the point. After a few attempts into his crackling walkie-talkie our newfound friend paused, frowned and then suddenly smiled and said, 'Okay!' while giving us the thumbs up. We responded with cheery 'Okays!' ourselves. He motioned for us to follow him and we filed out of the stadium behind him, just as Aaron Kwok was thanking the crowd, sending the girls into hysterics.

Back outside and running around the stadium's circumference, once again. Only this time, we had an armed policeman escorting us. We stopped short outside another entrance.

'Way hyuh,' he said in English, not Cantonese. It meant 'Wait here'. That much we understood. A short while later we saw Vera, Sonia and Porsche stumbling down the stairs and running in our direction! What relief! Two policemen had accompanied them as well, and the three sentinels now stood around laughing and clapping as if some great tragedy had been averted. We thanked the policemen profusely and then started making our way back in. Just as the guards were out of earshot, Vera spoke up.

'Guys, c'mon we have to make more of this. Let's find a way to get closer to the front rows before Tommy comes back on for the finale.'

'Exactly!' I agreed enthusiastically. 'I mean, I've come all the way here to meet Steffi, I've got to find her and get an autograph.'

'I saw a VIP entrance on our way here,' Sonia offered. 'You could tell, you know. There were TV vans and a red-carpet stairway.'

'What are we waiting for?' grinned Porsche. 'Let's go!'

'Oh you guys are going to get us arrested,' Avery grumbled but joined us all the same as we did an about-turn and sped off the way we had come. We sprinted in our heeled boots and were out of breath as we came upon the entrance, four gates down. Surprisingly, there was no one guarding the entrance, perhaps because the concert was clearly in its closing stages. We eased into a spotless marble corridor at the basement level that seemed to run across the entire width of the stadium. It was a bit overwhelming and we couldn't figure out what to do, so we just carried on towards the furthest end. Halfway there, a door labelled 'Engineering' opened and a tall Caucasian man stepped out, a clipboard in hand. He was startled to see us.

'Who're you?' he asked in a heavy American accent, looking as if he'd seen a ghost.

'Background dancers for Aaron Kwok,' Vera replied faster than lightning, a confident smile on her face.

He looked a bit unsure but then decided to let it go and carried on his way to another room. We all giggled silently. Our costumes were certainly coming in handy. Further down, we passed a door labelled 'Crew' and grinned at each other.

'Should we try and pretend to be the crew?' Alice asked, snatching the words out of my mouth.

Before we could debate on where to head next, the door opened, almost swiping my nose off. And standing there in front of me, dwarfing me by a good eight inches, was arguably the greatest female player in all of tennis history. I wanted to kiss her for want of anything better to do.

We looked at each other for a few seconds, she bemused, I stunned. Now what?

'Excuse me,' she said when I said nothing and motioned as if to try and get past us. But I didn't budge. This was Steffi Graf. This was why I was in China.

'I am a huge fan,' I said finally, mustering up the nerve to extend my palm for a handshake. Much more acceptable than a kiss. 'And it's such a pleasure to be able to meet you.'

Steffi smiled and shook my hand. The rest of the gang just stood around, silent spectators, taking in the extraordinary scene.

'Do you play tennis?' she asked.

'Yes, of course!' I answered animatedly. 'Tennis is my life!'

Just then, a man who was undoubtedly some sort of security personnel stepped out from behind the same door and took his position alongside her. Steffi was about to move off again, but I had one question.

'How do you keep wanting to win so bad, when you've already won it all, several times over?'

She paused at this, thought for a second and then spoke with a genuinely warm smile. 'Winning makes me happy. You just always have to do what makes you happy.'

As I registered this pearl of wisdom, Avery thankfully whipped out the autograph book that she had had the good sense to bring, and Steffi signed on reflex. Then she said goodbye to all of us and walked off lightning quick, the bodyguard close in step behind her.

'Oh my God!' was all I could manage to whisper.

'Oh my God!' Vera nearly screamed. 'How cool was that Tanya? Are you going to faint?'

'Listen girls, we'll have time to digest this later,' Sonia said, shaking me out of my stupor. 'Let's please try and get some of the other autographs that we came here for.'

Without another word we ran to the end of the corridor where Steffi had disappeared and here, we could hear the music incredibly loud. This last door had to lead into the backstage area, we collectively assumed, because the music sounded no more than twenty feet away. And it had been so easy. With a combined heave-ho we pushed through the door and were instantly struck dumb. We had blundered our way not back into the open, but into the VIP area, ahead of even the front rows. Seated there were Chinese aristocrats, politicians and Fraulein Graf herself! She turned to look at us in bewilderment and amusement. Two policemen started towards us at a deliberate pace. On our right, Tommy Rage was back on stage humming 'Your Shoulder To Cry On', oblivious of the commotion just an arm's length away from him.

'Run!' I cried out as the policemen closed in on us and to everyone's utter astonishment and shock, darted up the stairs onto the stage! Dumbfounded and flustered, my friends all ran after me in a dizzy mad rush and we found ourselves on stage, standing next to Tommy Rage. The guards might have also darted after us, but stopped short when they saw Tommy turn around to not only acknowledge us, but actually serenade us. He was used to screaming fans rushing onto stage, the Chinese police clearly weren't.

Those last few minutes of Tommy Rage's concert were pure bliss. We felt like we were in heaven. There we were, screaming and dancing on stage in white T-shirts and black waistcoats in front of a 3000-strong crowd, being serenaded by a famous pop star, watched by a tennis legend and fireworks going off in the background. Even I was induced into singing along as we joined in the chorus of 'Your Shoulder To Cry On'.

'Thank you!' Tommy Rage blew a kiss to the audience and the stadium erupted into applause and shrieks of 'Tommy! Tommy!'

A little curtsy bow in our direction and he disappeared backstage before we could grasp what happened. In a flash the guards were up on stage, grabbing us by the arms and leading us out of the VIP area. Steffi Graf was laughing. Ha! She'll remember me now for sure, I thought happily. Shutterbugs flashed away. The dream was over. As we were being dragged out, we wondered what was to become of us.

'Are we being arrested?' Porsche wondered out loud, echoing my thoughts.

'I warned you guys!' Avery snapped.

But mercifully, the police had nothing more in mind than shepherding us to the street, where remarkably, a sea of taxis had materialised.

'Can you guys believe what just happened?' Vera was laughing deliriously.

'Wait till we tell everyone about this!' Sonia squealed.

A couple of hours later, as I was the lone one left in the cab after dropping off Sonia, I steeled myself for what lay ahead. It was nearly three in the morning. Panic didn't begin to describe what I felt. A few tight slaps were undoubtedly par for the course, but what else? What was I going to do? What would I say? Any punishment would be worth it though; I had had the night of my life.

Popi and Shiny stood at the door as I tiptoed in, but didn't say a word.

'Where are they?' I asked.

'In their bedroom,' Shiny whispered back, solemnly. 'Do you know what the time is? Da, are you crazy?'

Gingerly, I walked over to the master-bedroom door. There was no point delaying the inevitable. But the lights were out.

'Are they asleep?' I looked at Shiny and Popi.

'No, they were awake just a few minutes ago. Try knocking.'

I knocked softly, then a little harder. No response. Just as I was about to call out to them and begin the long apology I had rehearsed in the taxi, I heard a giggle behind me. I turned around to find Popi and Shiny explode into laughter.

'What?' I exclaimed, incredulous. Could this mean what I thought it meant? 'Are they not home yet? That's not possible!'

Shiny and Popi's hysterical laughter confirmed it. My parents had miraculously not yet returned from their party and it was close to three in the morning! I couldn't believe my luck. This was just too good to be true.

'Da, you don't know how Popi and I have been freaking out,' Shiny chortled. 'After one o'clock, we thought you were dead. But they haven't shown up either!'

Just as I was about to indulge in some serious merrymaking by telling them all that had happened, the intercom buzzer rang. Shiny and I were off like a shot into our bedroom while Popi answered it. I dived into bed and pulled the quilt up to my chin. Shiny switched off the lights and pretended to be asleep. We heard them come in, say something to Popi about why she was wide-awake at this hour and then heard their footsteps towards their room.

And that was that. It was over. I had been all the way to China and back, danced on a stage, made Steffi Graf laugh, returned home in the wee hours of the morning and gotten away with it.

Ten

Valentine's Day

British-Malaysian Vera Locke was the one who had first pointed out the Charlton brothers to me, back in Fifth Form, as we stood against the railing of Court 1, watching the Senior Boys' Inter-house Volleyball final in progress. The Charlton boys were in blue, leading Nansen House, Colin the captain and Rudy his deputy. Masterpieces manufactured in the Anglo-Asian mixed-breed factory that Hong Kong was.

Already something of a PhD in the laws of attraction, Vera quipped quizzically, 'How come they aren't more popular than they are? I mean, look at them. They're gorgeous, they're super athletes and they're friendly with just about everyone. Why aren't more girls after them?'

I knew what she meant – despite possessing most of the pre-requisite criteria, they weren't exactly Blue Isle School royalty. In fact, neither of the two had a girlfriend as far as we knew and that was unheard of in jock-land. It suddenly dawned upon us that these were two plum catches readily available for the likes of us – middle class dwellers of the highly differentiated high school society. Jointly, we licked our lips. Unfortunately, we both decided to go after the same one: Rudy, the younger of the two siblings, who was also our batchmate.

'I mean, just look at those legs,' Vera whistled.

Grinning in concurrence I added, 'You bet. And don't miss that butt.'

Charged about our newfound challenge we both went about the next few weeks trying to hook Rudy Charlton for no reason other than him being an available ticket to the crème-de-la-crème of our social order.

If one day I'd bat my eyelids at him and ask for a few basketball tips after school, Vera would show up at the session with a platter of brownies that she supposedly baked herself. Yeah right. If I found Vera chatting with him during lunch break, I'd barge in on the conversation and flash my sweetest smile.

The whole thing was a highly entertaining charade to me, but Vera often did this – attacking a romantic interest with a formidable single mindedness of purpose. And she always got her man. It's a different matter that once she got him, she often didn't know what to do with him, sometimes ended up breaking a heart in the span of just two days and leaving us, her friends, to clean up the mess and make excuses on her behalf.

But Rudy Charlton was different and it didn't work. None of her impish flirtations, knockout looks, genuine affability or candid hints clicked with him for some reason. Not that mine did either. But I was least bothered and most amused that someone had finally shown immunity to Vera's charm. She of course, was indignant and maddened and after a few weeks of unsuccessfully trying to hook his attention, shrugged it off with the observation that he seemed too boring for her taste anyway. Sour grapes, anyone?.

My best friend had to leave Blue Isle School that winter, as Vera's family moved to Singapore and the Charlton brothers didn't cross my mind or my path until more than a year later. I had just entered Sixth Form, finally the summit of high-school. We didn't have to wear the school uniform anymore or attend more than three or four classes a day. Lower Sixth was when we were supposed to start preparing for the gruelling A-Level exams that lay at the end of Upper Sixth, but everyone wasted those 12 months away partying.

It was my first Biology lecture of the year and I was seated next to Sang-Kee in Lab 2, awaiting the enigmatic Mrs Lantz whom we had heard so much about. That was when Colin Charlton made his entrance, walking into class dribbling a basketball. He was really gorgeous, no denying that. Broad shoulders that would make a professional athlete envious, porcelain skin that seemed to be a birthright of all Eurasians, chiselled cheekbones, and narrow, intense Asian eyes. He beamed at Sang-Kee and me, then at the class in general and proceeded to seat himself at the desk adjacent to ours.

'Why is Colin Charlton in our class?' I leaned over and whispered to Sang-Kee. 'Isn't he in Upper Sixth?'

'Maybe he flunked,' she whispered back, but apparently not discreetly enough because Colin immediately replied from his seat.

'Hey, I didn't flunk,' he announced with a smile, causing Sang-Kee to turn a deep shade of beetroot. 'I only flunked Bio. I'm still in Upper Sixth, but I have to take double Bio to catch up.'

'It's much the same with me,' offered the boy he was seated next to. I looked up to find a very 'propah' looking English fellow, hair parted on the side, chequered sweater et al. 'I'm doing double Bio as well, and I'm in Upper Sixth. I'm new to Blue Isle anyway.' Then he stuck out his hand, far enough for me and Sang-Kee to be able to shake it. 'Hi, I'm Greg Campsey.'

Just as we were done exchanging introductions, Mrs Lantz walked in and automatically commanded absolute silence. She was olive-skinned and exquisite, with a mane of unruly black hair that she never attempted to tame. Her reputation preceded her – of being a tough taskmaster with a switchblade for a tongue.

Within a week or two, the repartee between Colin and me could no longer be described as just friendly banter. We were passing notes, stealing little glances at each other, exchanging shy smiles, teasing and ribbing. Sang-Kee and Greg were bemused bystanders as Colin and I flirted shamelessly through every Bio class. Mrs Lantz seemed to be well aware as well, and because she clearly liked me, gamely paired me with him for every dissection or chromatography. It suited Colin just fine, because I would do all the work and he would just sit there and smile that charming smile at me. Needless to say, the arrangement suited me just fine too.

During one class when a dozen unfortunate crabs were being cut open, Mrs Lantz stepped out to the staff-room for a while, while we were meant to get on with our business. Most of us did, but my partner asked permission to go out and play football instead. Considering I was the one granting the authorisation, he wasn't about to be denied. So off he went while I worked on the crustacean, although I would have much rather been playing football too. I was nearly done with the dissection when I looked up to see him hunkering in almost half an hour later, dripping in sweat, his shirt unbuttoned and flying open, revealing a washboard chest and six-pack abdomen. I had to actually gulp to keep an exclamation down.

'She's coming! Gimme the scalpel, quick!' he rushed over to my side.

I handed over the instruments to Colin, who immediately began an enthused charade of doing something with the crab.

'Maybe you should button up your shirt?' I suggested, for reasons other than the obvious. I couldn't hold my breath any longer and if I let go, I thought I might drool. He stared at me blankly for a moment and then looked down at himself and laughed.

'Oh shoot! I forgot about this,' he hollered and then looked at his hands, which thanks to not wearing the mandatory gloves, were now covered with crab. He turned towards me, the slyest grin plastered across his face. Uh-oh.

'I think you're going to have to do this, my dear,' he said with an astounding change in tone, leaning over close so I was barely inches from his chest. He raised his arms as if to indicate helplessness and I couldn't help a shy smile. Reluctantly, I took off my own gloves and with trembling fingers, started doing up his buttons. I could feel his breath on my hands. Somebody in the class whistled.

'Get a room!' someone else shouted. High school comics.

To my utter horror and embarrassment, Mrs Lantz walked in just as I was doing up the last button at his collar. I quickly left it and snapped my hands behind my back like a thief caught stealing. She stopped in her tracks and for a moment I thought she was going to explode into one of her famed eruptions. But she only raised an eyebrow, sucked in her cheeks in that sardonic Mrs Lantz smirk, and said, 'I don't want to know. As long as the dissection is done, I don't want to know.'

Colin's desk partner Greg also soon became good friends with Sang-Kee and me. He was really such a nice guy: well mannered, soft-spoken and sincerely good at heart. The kind that's not exactly hot property at sixteen, but someone any woman would give an arm and a leg for later in life.

'Why don't you just ask him out?' he would ask me about Colin.

'Why doesn't he?' I would always retort.

'He's too shy, never asked a girl out in his life.'

'Well I never asked anyone out either.'

I would learn later, that there is nothing more stupid than not acting upon a mutual attraction. *Carpe diem* should be everyone's motto when it comes to love and the like. But then I didn't take a step. It wasn't that I was shy, far from it; just that I had absolutely no clue what to do.

Meanwhile, on the platonic front, I had also become close friends with Victor Rose of the famed fanged smile. We'd met up last term on the school cross-country team and hit it off instantly. He was like my gay best friend, only he wasn't gay. He would advise me to dress more like a girl and less like a jock, and discuss the latest football and Formula One news with me. The first time I heard the name 'Michael Schumacher' was when he told me about the sensational new driver on the circuit. We also watched the disastrous San Marino Grand Prix together that year, the one that killed Ayrton Senna.

I would talk to Vicks about my crushes while he would discuss his, and the object of his affection was certainly never another boy. He was also bright, something which could not be said of most of my male colleagues from the athletics squad, and the two of us stayed up late talking on the phone, discussing everything from the abstract to the macabre. My highly disapproving mother was convinced this Vicks boy was my boyfriend and made no bones about her suspicions. I didn't know how to tell her that it was like accusing me of dating Vera, without her thinking Vicks was gay. So I just let her and her suspicions be.

The twist in the tale came when Vicks officially introduced me to his best friend, Rudy Charlton. Of course I already knew Rudy, but we started 'hanging out' only after I became friends with Victor. Along came Diwali night, a huge annual extravaganza at our cosmopolitan Blue Isle School and I convinced Vicks and his gang to attend it for the first time. There were food stalls, musical performances and arts and crafts. It was really good fun and Vicks showed up in high spirits, Zack Corrington and Rudy Charlton in tow. Zack and I had our history, but it was the other gentleman who stole my attention that evening.

Up close, Rudy Charlton was striking. Not only was he good looking, but also poised, reticent and intelligent, quite unlike his elder brother. There was something else, a certain *je ne sais quoi*. He was the kind of man who had one of the two effects on women: either they began to flirt involuntarily, or, they just crashed to a shutdown.

After several minutes of bombarding him with questions and receiving only monosyllabic responses, I decided I was not going to crash.

'Why don't you talk?' I asked. Evidently I had not discovered subtlety just yet.

'I don't feel the need to,' he replied, with a shrug of the shoulder and then, with an indulgent smile, added, 'You're doing enough talking for the two of us.'

I blushed and in a flash understood why Vera's particular brand of flirtation hadn't worked with this guy, almost two years ago. He was mature beyond his years. I was so overwhelmed that I had to run to the school phone to call Sang-Kee, with the kind of urgency you have when you really need to run to the loo.

'What do I do?' I shouted into the phone, even as '*choli ke peechhe*' came on the loudspeakers, sounding completely out of place outside our Welsh principal's office. 'Sang-Kee, I feel like I've been hit by a truck, I haven't felt this kind of crush since . . . since Zack Corrington. And you know how long ago that was.'

Sang-Kee laughed and said it would probably pass. 'It had better. Because people are already beginning to talk about Colin and you.'

Oh yes, Rudy was Colin's brother. Okay, so this is what they call a sticky situation. I decided to follow Sang-Kee's advice: 'this too shall pass.' But Vicks, Rudy and I started hanging out a lot after that.

One day as we lounged around in the Wilberforce common room, Rudy walked over casually and asked if I'd seen any movies lately.

'Not really, not in a while,' I replied. 'My friends are the most boring people in the world. They only want to watch movies like *Sleepless in Seattle* and *What's Love Got to Do with It*.'

'And you?' he asked, raising an intrigued eyebrow.

'Well,' I fidgeted a bit, embarrassed to disclose my peculiar choice in films. 'I'd rather go see that new Sylvester Stallone film.'

'*Demolition Man*!' Rudy nearly jumped out of his chair, laughing. 'Are you serious?'

I didn't know whether to retract my statement by pretending it was a joke or to stand my ground. I did neither.

'That's brilliant,' he said. 'Do you want to go see it today?'

My heart stopped. Here it is, I thought. This is a date; he's just asked me out on a date. And he doesn't think I'm a weirdo for wanting to watch a brainless action film. But to my dismay Vicks, who was in the vicinity, promptly and thoughtlessly invited himself along. I guess that proves he was heterosexual. A gay friend would have intuitively known when three is a crowd.

But the crowd went to the movies alright, because unfortunately Vicks wasn't gay. As we entered the multiplex at Pacific Place, a clown stood at the red carpeted entrance with a bunch of helium balloons in his hand, obviously meant for children heading towards Dennis the Menace. To my surprise, Rudy cheerfully picked a couple and fondly handed them to me, as if I were a child. I should have been outraged, but instead I felt thrilled like a silly little girl. It was like falling in love with a much older man, only he wasn't.

That New Year's Eve a bunch of us went out to paint the town red. By then I had managed to convince Sang-Kee that Vicks was falling for her, and told Vicks in no uncertain terms that she had her eyes on him. He was excited; she was flattered – the plan seemed to be working well. We had a few beers in the nightclub district of Lan Kwai Fong – illegally of course, we were just 16 – and then rounded up on a secluded balcony at Alexandra House Mall to drink some more and play Truth or Dare.

After a while Vicks and Sang-Kee went to 7-Eleven's to get more beers. Alice and a couple of others excused themselves and went looking for loos. All of a sudden, it was down to just Rudy and me, and I swiftly realised the situation had been brought about by design. What considerate friends we had! There we were on that dimly lit balcony, the brilliant lights of Queensway Plaza shimmering far below us. A distant cacophony of revellers counting down to the New Year, people thronged by the thousands in nearby Lan Kwai Fong. It was magical. I didn't know what to say or do, since I'd never been in such a position before. Surely someone had to make the first move? So I casually put my head onto his shoulder, and immediately he put his arm around me, welcoming my gesture.

This was it, I thought. Was this going to be my first real kiss? My heart was racing at 150 beats a minute, but I acted as though I was almost sleepy. Rudy shifted his weight, a firecracker went off in the distance and I knew this was it, any moment now.

'HAPPY NEW YEAR!!'

Vicks and Sang-Kee came bouncing back into the picture like a badly timed joke, juggling several cans of Budweiser. So it hadn't been thoughtful design after all. But I was in too good spirits to let it disappoint me much. There would be many, many more such moments, I was confident of that.

The New Year brought with it many changes. For one, Vicks asked Sang-Kee out on the very first day of the year and despite my satisfaction at having played Cupid successfully, I couldn't help feel a tinge of envy because nothing was official about Rudy and me just yet. Or about Colin and me for that matter.

Oh yes, I continued to flirt with Colin but mostly only in reciprocation. He was too adorable to rebuff and besides, he had not given me any reason to behave otherwise. To top it all, he looked like Keanu Reeves for God's sake; what was a girl supposed to do? And so it continued. Biology class and after-school socialisation were such far-removed worlds that I thought no one would ever be the wiser. It also helped that the two brothers had a serious sibling rivalry problem and barely spoke to each other. They were always trying to go one up on the other. If one led the school football team, the other skippered rugby and volleyball. If Rudy managed good grades, Colin looked like a movie star. Their lives were far apart and I played it to my advantage. I felt like some sort of female Casanova and was on a perpetual high. Vera would have been proud.

But neither brother was taking that final step. So I decided I had to. Valentine's Day was coming around in just about two weeks and

I would ask the man of my dreams out through Einstein House's messenger service. The only problem was that I now had to choose, once and for all. And I also knew that it had to be Rudy. For all of Colin's gorgeousness and congeniality, he wasn't the one that made my heart skip beats. I would have loved to go out with him, if only I had never met his brother. So, after much deliberation with Sang-Kee, I finally wrote the message and popped it in the box that stood outside the principal's office.

Dear Rudy,

We've had so many wonderful moments together. I know we share something special that we both feel, so don't you think it's about time to put a name to it? Be my Valentine.

Tanya

I was thrilled to bits and looking forward to a glorious period as the girlfriend of Blue Isle School football captain Rudy Charlton. Of course, there was still the matter of preparing Colin for what lay ahead, and simply withdrawing my flirtations wasn't going to cut it. I tried to be brusque, I tried to drop hints but he was Colin, you see, and simply didn't catch on. And he was just so sweet. He'd bring me a wildflower from the wooden steps that led down the hill behind the school, and I would lose my resolve. He'd wink at me in the middle of one of Mrs Lantz's outbursts and cause me to laugh out loud. He really was such a darling that I couldn't bring myself to tell him.

Meanwhile Rudy was noticeably cooling off and I couldn't for the life of me imagine why. He was returning fewer phone calls and making no plans after school. I quizzed Vicks about it, but Mr Rose was so lost in the throes of his new romance that he claimed absolute ignorance about his best friend's life. Vicks and Sang-Kee were getting on my nerves. They were always in each other's face and never had time for anyone else in the world. I had, by cleverly playing Cupid, forfeited the time and attention of two of my closest friends. Their phone lines were perpetually engaged as if they spoke to each other 24 hours a day. Perhaps they did. What did I know? I, who had never had a boyfriend? But boy, was that status about to change soon.

If only I knew.

That Saturday morning, I received a phone call from a very grave sounding Alice.

'Have you heard?' she said, getting straight to the point in characteristic style.

'Heard what?' I asked, stunned by the tone of her voice. Had somebody died?

'About Rudy and Deirdre?'

The mention of a female name in the same breath as Rudy's caused my heart to sink. This was not going to be good. With a lump in my throat, I managed to whisper, 'No, what about Rudy and Deirdre?'

There was an uncomfortable silence at the other end and immediately I knew it was probably even worse than I had thought. Finally Alice took a heavy breath and spoke.

'Rudy got off with Deirdre last night,' she said solemnly, allowing the words to sink into my head.

My first thought was denial. It wasn't possible. Rudy, the reticent, chivalrous fellow who couldn't even bring himself to kiss me when he could have, making out with a girl without even asking her out? And that too, the pasty and podgy racist piglet Deirdre Bradshaw?

'How do you know?' I finally found my voice, but the words were strained. 'Who told you?' Maybe the source was some gossipmonger like Porsche, whose scraps of information were always dubious.

'I was there.'

'What do you mean? Where were you?'

'We went out last night, a whole bunch of us. Deirdre and her friends were there too, and Rudy and Zack. Everyone had a bit too much to drink. For what it's worth, she practically forced herself upon him, I swear, I was right there. And he was smashed out of his skull.'

As if that somehow made it excusable. Anger and hurt shot up inside me. It felt like Rudy had cheated on me. Only, the even more exasperating fact was that I had absolutely no legitimate claim to him. Aching with confusion and rage, I lashed out at Alice, for want of a better target.

'You went out last night with Rudy and his friends and didn't even have the decency to call and invite me?'

Alice was brusque enough to make me madder. 'It was mostly my art class gang, you barely even know them. I didn't know Rudy and Zack were going to be there until we got to the restaurant. In fact Zack even suggested I call you, but it was so late by then and I know your mother . . .' She left the rest unsaid. The world and its uncle knew that Indian parents didn't allow their teenagers out at late hours, without prior permission.

I was heartbroken and struggled to get through the rest of the weekend. I didn't want to call him – this was not something I was going to discuss over the phone. It had to wait till Monday. My only fear was that Rudy might actually ask Deirdre out sometime before then, you know, make an honest woman of her. Well, so be it then, I thought. If he wanted to ask her out, there wasn't much I could do about it.

First thing Monday morning, before classes started, I marched over to the Nansen common room and demanded to see Rudy outside, in the corridor. He sauntered over casually as if nothing had happened.

'Can we talk in private please?' I asked gruffly, looking pointedly at the 6 foot 7 inch Simon Fennel, who stood there, smirking in the doorway. Simon looked exactly like a certain seventeen-year-old cricketer named Andrew Flintoff, who across a few seas, was making a sensational debut for Lancashire the very same season.

'I don't think there's anything we need to discuss that can't be said in public,' Rudy replied, looking me squarely in the eye, insolently, as if I was the one who had done something wrong. I couldn't believe his cheek. What was wrong?

'All right then, if you want the world to know,' I shot back, equally terse. 'I thought we had something. What's this about Deirdre? How could you?'

'That's none of your business,' he said coolly and it felt like a slap. Nothing in my life had ever hurt more. *None of my business?* Why was I being treated like this, and that too in public? What had I done to deserve this? I got my answer immediately.

'As for how could I, well, maybe you should ask yourself that,' Rudy continued, now looking visibly upset. 'What did you think? That I was never going to find out about you and Colin? You think I'm stupid, that I live on some other planet?'

Instant humiliation walloped me into a shocked silence. I couldn't believe he knew. How long had he known? All of a sudden, Rudy's recent behaviour made a lot of sense. I could no longer meet his gaze, and hung my head in shame, my cheeks burning. I wanted the ground to swallow me up. There was nothing I could say in my defence because his accusations were a hundred percent true. But even so, I didn't want to lose him, I liked him so much.

'Rudy, it's not what you think, Colin . . . ' I struggled to speak or look him in the eye. 'Colin and me are just friends.'

Rudy deliberately looked the other way and said nothing, while Simon Fennel watched with such glee it made me think he must hate me.

And then my next horrified thought was, 'Does Colin also know?'

Shamelessly enough, I asked Rudy that. And the look in his eyes told me that any shreds of sentiment he might have still had left were wiped out instantly.

'No, he's too thick to look beyond his own fingers and toes,' he said with disgust and walked away.

'What are you going to do now?' giant Simon asked, grinning at me, thoroughly enjoying the real-life soap opera unfolding before him.

'I'm going to kill myself,' I said dejectedly, almost meaning it.

'Can I watch?' Fennel said, delighted.

Broken-hearted and despondent, I found refuge, as always, on the tennis court. For the next few days, I would bide my time until the last class and then rush off to the courts to thrash whoever was unfortunate enough to be standing across the net. Had I been able to sustain those emotions for the next five years, I might even have won Wimbledon. But Raquel Del Rosario's party that weekend proved to be the start of another course.

Being invited to a senior's party was the same as having your social stock skyrocket. So I was delighted at the invitation – an opportunity to do something other than pine for my lost love. I also knew Colin would be there. It was like gate-crashing a rock stars' party. All the bold and beautiful people from the top-rung in the school were present, including the school head-girl Morgan Smith who was making quite an intoxicated spectacle of herself in the middle of the dance floor. Someone else was already passed out on the carpet. The syrupy odour of hash hung heavy in the air, only back then I didn't quite know what that peculiar smell was. What a difference a year made. These seniors were not just trying desperately to get as high as possible — which is mostly what my peers did at a party — they were elevated to another plane altogether.

After exhausting ourselves on the dance floor, Colin and I found a quiet spot out on the tiny balcony adjoining the living room.

We were still panting from the frenzied dancing when he slipped his hand over mine on the wooden balustrade. I turned to look at him and our eyes locked for a few moments. And then, without a word, he leaned in and kissed me.

Shooting stars went off in my head and I felt such a rush I thought I might faint. He tasted sweet, of orange juice and mint. It was wonderful.

When we re-entered the party, red-faced and self-conscious, Greg smiled at us from across the room. As soon as Colin left my side for a minute, Greg rushed over to me and gave me a tight hug.

'I'm so happy for you two!' he whispered, beer on his breath. 'It's finally happening, *hallelujah!*'

He also told me that Colin was going to officially ask me out the very next day — Valentine's Day. He had sent me a Valentine to say as much. All of a sudden, a dreadful thought struck me, making the music disappear and the world go blank. Horrified, I remembered that my own Valentine addressed to Rudy Charlton would be making its way to him the next morning. I had completely forgotten about that! I must have gone white as a ghost because Greg asked me what was wrong. But I didn't have the guts to tell him; I felt like a worm. There was only one thing to do – I would have to find someone in Einstein House first thing in the morning, and pull a few strings before Form Period started.

But as luck would have it, it rained cats and dogs on the morning of the 14th of February that year and the 6A school bus broke down en route. Never, but never, does that happen among Hong Kong's aristocratic British school buses. It was as if some higher power was pulling out all stops to make sure I got what I deserved. Another bus was promptly dispatched to fetch us from Caine Road, where we were stranded, but by then I knew it would all be over.

I walked listlessly into the common room where Form Period was in progress and Mr Stern sat there, smiling brightly at me. He informed me that I had a very special rose waiting for me. He might as well have told me I was dead. I walked up to his desk, picked up the rose and the whole class cooed and chuckled as I opened the accompanying message.

> *To the smartest and most interesting girl I know,*
> *Will you be my Valentine, my girlfriend and my 'biology' instructor*
> *4 ever?*
>
> *Love,*
> *Colin*

In spite of myself, I had to smile at the juvenile use of quotation marks around the word biology. It was classic Colin, daft to the point of being crude, yet childlike enough to be adorable. I bit my lip and actually fought an urge to cry. I didn't know what was to happen next, almost didn't care. I resigned myself to fate, the way a man walking towards the electric chair probably gives in to vast hopelessness. I wasn't even worried anymore. Bring it on, I felt like shouting at fate.

As I packed my things to leave for the class, I saw Greg standing at my Form Room door, glowering. A sharp pain hit me in the pit of my stomach.

'What is wrong with you?' he practically bellowed at me, unmindful of all the passers-by. He didn't have to elucidate any further; we both knew exactly what he was talking about.

Colin had apparently announced to his entire class that he was expecting a Valentine from me, his girlfriend from that day on. When no Valentine arrived, he gamely shrugged off the ribbing of his classmates, but once Form Period broke up, news travelled fast from Rudy's common room next door and someone informed Colin that his brother had received a Valentine from his supposed 'girlfriend'. I was mortified, this was even worse than I had imagined. I wanted to turn to dust and disappear.

'Colin is the laughing stock of the whole of Nansen House, and very soon, the whole school.' Greg snapped, barely able to contain his temper. 'Can you please explain this, because I'm obviously missing something here.'

It was too much to explain. He wouldn't understand anyway. No one would. So I just told him that I'm a horrible person and to tell Colin that I was really, really sorry. Greg walked off in disgust. A few of my classmates were standing around, relishing the show.

'Did you send a Valentine to Rudy Charlton?'

'But you got one from Colin Charlton?'

'Ha! That's the most hilarious thing I've ever heard,' Zack Corrington laughed the loudest, forever jealous of my romantic interest in anybody other than himself. I glared at him and he had the good sense to stop chortling. I bunked Bio that day, something

I had never done before, and hid in the library for the better part of two hours. I needn't have. Sang-Kee informed me at lunch that Colin had cut the class too, for obvious reasons. I truly, honestly wanted to disappear off the face of the Earth. The rest of the day went by in an aching blur and I practically dashed to the school bus when the bell went. Sinking low in my seat at the back, I wished Sonia – my usual bus mate – wouldn't be on the bus. Everybody had heard about the scandal by then, and I was in no mood to provide juicy details to any curious soul. So I sank even lower into my seat and pretended I was sick. No one bothered the villain the rest of the way home.

I had barely entered the house when the phone rang like it would fly off the hook. Mum never appreciated the ringing when one of her private English tuitions were on, so I hastily flung my bag aside and ran to answer it.

'You won't believe what's happening!' Sang-Kee was shouting at the other end. There was a loud commotion behind her.

'Where are you?' I shouted back, catching a stern glance from my mother and an inquisitive look from her 6-year-old student Jai Koo. I lowered my voice. 'What's going on?'

Sang-Kee was in hysterics and I couldn't tell if she was laughing or crying. 'I'm still at school. They're beating each other up!'

'Who?' I asked, alarmed. What was she talking about?

'Colin and Rudy, they're bashing each other's brains out on the volleyball court! Half the school seems to be here, this is crazy!'

'Where's coach Bailey?' I was stunned and shouting again, ignoring my mother's now very irritated expression. There were more important things going on in the world.

'Who cares where Mr Bailey is?' Sang-Kee yelled back. 'Are you mad? Did you hear what I said? You're a rock star! The two brothers are fighting over you — now that's what I call a compliment.' She was laughing again and despite the shocking news, vanity forced a smile out of me.

Rudy never spoke to me again, while Colin, incredibly enough, remained the sweetheart that he was. After a few obligatory days of awkwardness, he resumed his silly jokes and pleasant demeanour to my immense delight and relief. Hats off to him, he turned out to be a bigger man than I had thought and I genuinely fell in love with him after that. But needless to say, it was too late. The week after that fateful Valentine's Day, he asked the vapid Sheena Harhuis out. Any other girl would have been self-conscious enough, knowing she had been picked up as a classic rebound, but not the Dutch space-cadet Ms Harhuis. She fawned over Colin in public and showed him off like a trophy, especially around me, making me squirm. Not that I didn't deserve it. I had learnt well enough why they say a bird in hand is worth two in the bush, and never tried such a stunt again.

Well, never to get caught at least!

Eleven

Step by Step

The first thing that hits you about India when you return after a prolonged absence is not the clammy air, the swarming crowds or even the obsession with cricket, it's the damn car horns and the drivers that use them indiscriminately, breaking traffic signals at will, verbally venting their many frustrations through rolled-down windows, generating a perpetual, bizarre cacophony.

As I ventured out from the austere environs of the IGI airport into a land that was once home, now alien, it is this phenomenon that stunned me into a cowered silence for the first few minutes. Thankfully, the Delhi Punjabis have discovered the loudest car stereos on the planet – if it weren't for Bhangra Pop blaring from every Maruti and Honda, the entire population could go positively insane. Better deaf than nuts.

We were back for good and pretty pleased about it too. Despite an exhilarating life in Hong Kong we had genuinely missed India.

Distance does make the heart grow fonder and the passage of time, fonder still. Shiny and I remembered only family weddings and Hindi music – the good stuff. India was almost beginning to acquire a mythical, romantic quality. Another year or two away and we might have begun believing in levitating swamis and the great Indian rope trick.

So when Papa informed us that his deputation posting was nearing its end and that he was expecting transfer orders soon, we both reacted with cheerful enthusiasm instead of despair, much to his surprise.

'We'll be with Kartik and Saurav again!'

'We won't have to miss a single family wedding now!'

We even believed 'we'll be able to keep a dog,' for some reason. Pity, that.

Since it was not clear when exactly Papa's transfer orders would arrive, it was decided that Shiny and me be sent off immediately as both of us were in our Board Exam years – she preparing for her GCSEs and me for my A-Levels. So calls were made, correspondence exchanged and the two of us were to be transferred into The British Embassy School in New Delhi starting November that year. It all sounded so exciting – fun, family and frolic in India, just like the good old times. So we bade our goodbyes, attended farewell parties and vowed to keep in touch with close friends forever. And then, we were off.

It was just Kartik and Saurav to receive us at the airport; that was the first pleasant surprise. Kartik was now seventeen, sported long sideburns and a leather jacket, and looked striking. Saurav, sporting Adidas gear was unmistakably a keen sportsman – he had the peculiar tan and inimitable shoulders that only the more athletically inclined could possess. They drove their own car and were considered responsible enough to fetch us from the airport.

'Just you guys? How cool is that?' I said, hugging the two of them together.

We were ecstatic at being together again, the four of us, and as we loaded the baggage into Kartik's Landcruiser we chatted non-stop, trying to catch up on all the years gone by. Bollywood music blared on his speakers as Kartik drove like the wind and we all sang along at the top of our voices like idiots. Kartik then lit up a cigarette and I was shocked and impressed at the same time.

'Do you want a puff?' he asked in my direction.

Why the hell not, I thought. This felt like freedom.

We were taken directly to the house in Hauz Khas that we still thought of as Gashaji's home, but was now inhabited by my father's parents. Sadly, he had passed away while we were in Hong Kong and Shiny and I had not been able to accompany our parents for his cremation, due to school, the expense and such inadequate reasons. It was one of the regrets that both of us held in our hearts, that we had not been able to say goodbye to our favourite – Gashaji. So it felt very strange when we walked in: the entire Trivedi clan congregated to welcome us, my father's parents running the household, their staid furniture that had once belonged in Lucknow having replaced poor Gashaji's eccentric collection of museum relics and *objets d'art*. But we didn't get much of an opportunity to let it sink in – we were overwhelmed by excited relatives, all talking at the same time, hugging, kissing and even pinching our cheeks. Everyone was more interested in our British accents and Chinese haircuts than the fact that we were genuinely glad to be back.

'You've turned into such a pretty girl!' one uncle said with such astonishment in his voice that I felt like responding, 'Well, did you expect me to remain ugly and fat for the rest of my life?' Of course, I left that unsaid and only smiled politely.

That night, as Shiny and I went to bed, we felt the first wave of real gloom. Gashaji should have been there; the place was incomplete without him. And it finally started sinking in that we really had left it all behind – Blue Isle School, the sitcom life, our friends, everything we had known and loved over the past half-decade.

'I hope this is going to turn out well,' Shiny said in the dark, echoing my thoughts. Before I could reply, the fan switched itself off.

'What was that?' Shiny jumped and caught my arm. We both had the same feeling instantly – that Gashaji was there, trying to communicate with us. Utter silence, not a wisp of air. *Badi ma,* our Hitler-like grandmother came shuffling into the room in the black stillness.

'Light *gayi,*' she informed us, and it took us a moment to register her comment.

'Huh?'

'The electricity is gone, it usually takes an hour or two to be back,' she told us. 'Try and go back to sleep.'

Electricity. An elusive mistress in the capital city. I had forgotten about that. Oh well, I thought, it wasn't Gashaji after all. We were settling back into bed when Shiny screamed.

'Da! There's something on my pillow!' and she was off the bed like a shot.

I slipped off my side of the bed and hopped across to the door that opened onto the veranda. The old door creaked open and with it came a fresh gust of wind. I looked back at Shiny, who was now faintly discernable, a quivering, shaking silhouette. There definitely was something on her pillow, I could see that now. About six inches long, and dark.

'It's a lizard,' I said as calmly as possible, so as not to upset her too much, but my stomach shrank. It had, after all, been several years since I had encountered a reptile in my bedroom. I gingerly picked up the pillow and tried to tap the creature off behind the bed. It decided to leap onto my arm instead.

I screamed.

Shiny screamed.

Then *badi ma* screamed, as she ran back into our room.

The lizard, clearly terrified by now, jumped off my arm.

'What happened? What happened?' *Badi ma* panted, knocking over the bedside lamp and phone.

'There was a lizard on our bed,' Shiny said, still shaking.

'A lizard?' was all *badi ma* said and without any further inquiry or reassurance, stumbled her way out of our room. As if to suggest that a lizard was hardly reason enough for such pandemonium.

'You can sleep on my side if you want,' I said, feeling sorry for Shiny.

'Thanks, Da,' she said meekly and morosely walked over to the other side of the bed.

We lay there quietly and sadly for a good two hours, wide awake, listening to the crickets out in the garden and involuntarily picturing other creatures slowly surrounding our bed.

Welcome back to India, the lizard had declared.

The British Embassy School, thankfully, was more familiar territory. Most of the students were diplomats' children, many of them Indian but from varied backgrounds. The first Monday I attended felt like homecoming, more so because I was crowned instant royalty for some curious reason; every guy tried to start a conversation with me, each popular girl made a bid to welcome me into her fold. I had no idea why, but it was amusing, unexpected and thoroughly welcome. Within two days I had a posse, a social life and even a best friend – Mullica, the undisputed queen bee and party animal. She and I became thick quickly and assumed the title of the Snake Sisters, a sorority of sorts that essentially required members to act snooty, dress sexy, spit venom and flash the fake snake tattoos on our thighs, which we painstakingly applied every morning.

Amazingly and expediently enough, Mullica lived alone as her parents were still in Bulgaria. So I spent practically half my life at Mullica's, away from the claustrophobic confines of my autocratic grandmother's house sucked into a life of reckless decadence. Mullica's abode was the non-stop party destination where the revelry never ended, it simply continued from one hazy evening to the next foggy dawn, days going by in a blur.

It was during this time that my first official boyfriend arrived and departed, but I was in such a stupor that I barely even noticed. He was a theatre actor called Milan, who had the misfortune of landing up for one of our famed parties. I knew I had his attention during Dumb Charades, as I enacted a convincing rendition of Jamie Lee Curtis' pole dance in True Lies. More than one pair of eyes followed me around after that, but he was the cutest of the lot; by the end of the evening, we were dancing in each other's arms. Before the gathering broke up, we had kissed and he had asked me out.

'Baby! You're even faster than me!' Mullica slurred and whispered into my ear, while Milan and I made a spectacle of ourselves on the couch.

'Wake up, Milan's here,' Mullica said and winked at me as she tried to rouse me barely four hours after the party had concluded.

Hung-over and sleepy, I buried my head in the pillow and mumbled something about not wanting to be disturbed. But then I caught sight of him standing in the doorway, grinning like an overeager sheepdog with a bouquet of roses cradled in his arm. Why didn't I feel as excited as he looked?

'Hi,' I managed to say with a forced smile when all I wanted to do was go back to sleep. 'You're up early.'

Mullica exited the scene, allowing Milan to come over and sit by my bedside. Self-consciously I pushed my hair away from my face and tried to sit up. Before I could, he leaned over and kissed me passionately. I felt nothing. In fact, with less alcohol running in my veins, he wasn't even all that cute.

'This is such a lucky house,' he said, placing the flowers in my hands.

'Why?' I asked, intrigued. Perhaps he had experienced more than a couple of interesting encounters at Mullica's pad. Or maybe this place was famous for bringing couples together.

'Because I met you here!' he said indignantly, affronted that I hadn't caught on immediately. I almost gagged. What was this, Santa Barbara?

'We've not even known each other for twenty-four hours.' I felt like screaming at him, but said nothing and tried to smile. Was this what relationships were about: you get drunk, you make out and then you tolerate each other forever after?

I tried to give it a shot, I really did. We went out for movies and dinners, met every other evening for a stroll in Deer Park. But by trying too hard to please, Milan bored me to tears in one week flat and by the end of the second week I would pass the phone on to Shiny every time he called, telling her to carry on the conversation pretending to be me. She actually complied too, never letting on to the poor chap what a joke he had become. A few days later though, I had no choice but to pull the plug.

It was a frigid December day and we were at Chona's in Khan Market. I was actually not dying of boredom for a change. Animatedly, I was telling him about the new ruling from the European Court of Justice that threatened to shake European football to its very foundations. European clubs would no longer be restricted from signing foreign players and players were also going to be entitled to a free transfer at the end of their contracts. The implications were huge and I was excited.

Out of the blue Milan said, 'You know, I'm the luckiest guy.' Smiling like the cat that got the cream, he grasped my hands into his. 'My wife is going to watch sport with me.'

'Excuse me?' I burnt both our hands as I spilled my hot chocolate. He yelped and pulled his hand back.

'What? Did I say something wrong?'

'You said *wife*,' I replied, too shocked to elucidate further.

'So?' he asked, an accusatory look descending into his eyes. 'We are going to get married, aren't we?'

'Are you crazy?' I stood up and the entire restaurant turned to watch. 'We're only seventeen!'

'I'm not saying we'll get married today,' he panicked, looked around at all the eyes trained in our direction and pulled me back down to sit. 'We'll wait till we're twenty-one,' he whispered manically.

All right, this did it. This guy was living so much in denial he wouldn't acknowledge it if I punched him in the face.

'Milan, are you blind? Are you deaf? Are you stupid?' I couldn't hold it in any longer. 'Do you not *notice* that I'm really mean to you?'

'What are you talking about? I love you.'

I slapped my forehead in frustration but felt immediately sorry for him. He was a nice guy, just not the one for me. My tone softened but what I had to say was inevitable.

'But I don't. Don't you *see* that?'

And I ran for my life.

In any case, Milan had been incidental. The real interest I had developed by this time was in my classmate Sam. Sam Naidu was the distinctive tall, dark and handsome type, sporty as well as half-German. That was the icing on the cake. Now the problem was that he was already seeing someone. His girlfriend of one year was Saira, the president of the World Bimbos Union – with a 36 DD bust and skinny legs to match. And they really did seem to be in love. So reluctantly, I resigned myself to the fact that my love life, which had of late acquired the speed of a Concorde, would once again slow down to a snail's pace.

But I hadn't counted on two things. One: it is a universal rule that the first boyfriend takes forever to arrive, but after that they just start falling into your lap. And two: a marvel named Nisha and her ten-step guide.

Nisha was Shiny's classmate, half-Indian and half-French. You would think such a genetic recipe would have produced a stunner, but it hadn't really. Nisha was somewhat plump, dressed like a hippy and wouldn't compel you to look twice if you passed her on the road. But this mademoiselle was a champion at *affaires de cœur*. She had all the boys eating out of her hands, besotted, and love-struck. I would see her in the cafeteria at lunch time, surrounded by her fan-following, posturing like a princess, hypnotised attendants in waiting fawning over her. Her *modus operandi* puzzled me, but it was the day she bagged the prized scalp of Katanga – the boy every girl in school wanted — that I was downright flabbergasted. He was the Sudanese ambassador's son — tall, handsome and athletic as well as intelligent, witty and downright charming. Mr Perfect.

Shock waves rippled through the school that Friday afternoon as Katanga dumped his existing girlfriend Lucy — a redhead Polish bombshell — and asked Nisha out. Some girls from his class went into post-traumatic shock, others into clinical depression if you took their word for it. I, of course was not the least bit interested, but I was impressed all right. How does she do it, I asked Shiny. How does Nisha get whichever guy she wants, whenever she pleases?

A fateful sequence of incidents unfolded thereafter as Shiny was blunt enough to relay my question verbatim to Nisha, who in turn was sporting enough to let us in on her secret. Life was never the same again for either of us.

'Do you remember Sharon Stone in Basic Instinct?' Nisha asked a bewildered Shiny. 'She says, "men are the easiest animals to tame." Well darling, it's true.'

There was a method evidently, a carefully constructed 10-step guide, which if devoutly followed, was allegedly foolproof. And over the next few weeks I committed it to memory for life.

'Number one: Guys like girls who are nice to them,' Nisha informed Shiny and me listening with the rapt attention of good disciples. We were seated under the banyan tree outside the cafeteria, munching on Snickers. 'So if you think you should act pricey and cool, please throw that attitude out of the window. It'll get you nowhere. Neither will shyness.'

'But aren't guys supposed to like girls who play hard to get and all that?' Shiny asked, her danglers reflecting the afternoon sun. The orthodontic treatment over the past one year had delivered, and Shiny had metamorphosed into a beauty.

'Hogwash,' came the reply. 'They may lust after them, but they won't have the balls to ask them out. Guys propose to girls who they think are going to say yes. So be nice, help the kid out a bit. Give your crush a chance to discover what a nice person you are.'

'Don't worry, you don't really have to be one. You just make him think you are,' I naughtily added with a wink and Nisha laughed in wholehearted agreement.

Armed with this new information, I set about becoming better friends with Sam. I always greeted him in the hallway, discussed the latest match scores and invited him to join my friends and me for movies, along with Saira of course. It was important for her not to perceive me as a threat just yet, so she wouldn't withdraw his availability. And it began to work. Sam and I indulged in increasingly longer conversations, discovered common interests and began to get along like a house on fire.

Then it was time for step two.

'You have to make sure you proceed to step two well before you become as comfortable as an old sweatshirt to him. Bring out the lipsticks and the perfume. And then start with the glances. Not dreamy or yearning ones but quick, pert and cheeky ones. Have fun.'

I would let Sam 'accidentally' catch me looking at him and break off the glance with a sweet smile, not an embarrassed expression. According to Nisha, any guy would skip a heartbeat. But not if your expression is self-conscious, or if the glance itself is too lovelorn. Then, an alarm will go off in his head, telling him to run. No, I had to find the right balance and it wasn't so difficult. I just had to look confident and happy. That's all.

'Now, a problem might arise if he takes the bait too soon, but you can't let it happen just yet. You want him to fall harder. So you shouldn't act too interested if he responds quickly, which he's likely to do because he's a guy. But you've got to confuse him. Nothing better than a mystery to unravel.'

Sam did start reciprocating almost immediately, but Nisha had wisely instructed me to pull back a bit, as per step three. So I flirted all right, but never seriously. It was all in good fun, laughed off with a few chortles and I also made it a point to flirt with other guys in his presence. Even though I was thoroughly enjoying this ridiculous charade, I was sceptical – such contrived behaviour couldn't possibly work. But the more I played along, the more it actually did. Enlightening.

Next, I was told, I must become friends with his friends. 'Make sure they think you're fabulous,' Nisha would tell us. 'Guys really are pack animals, their likes and dislikes are the same as their friends. So if his friends start thinking of you as super, chances are, he will too.'

And so, right on cue, I went about becoming great friends with Sam's closest buddies Sunil and Sudipto. I probably would have befriended them in any case – they were terrific guys and I genuinely liked them. But yes, I made that progressing camaraderie only too apparent, to Sam.

One Saturday morning as Sam and I were hitting a few balls on the clay courts at the Siri Fort Sports Complex, I decided to put Nisha's fourth step into execution. Apparently it was time to drop a hint, even at the cost of behaving like a bimbo.

As we both approached the net to retrieve a few balls, I asked Sam point blank whether or not he was in love with Saira.

'Of course I am,' he replied, looking up, a quizzical expression on his bronzed face. 'I've been seeing her for almost a year. But why do you ask?'

'Well, someone wants to know,' I said playfully, a glint of mischief in my eye and a cheeky smile on my lips.

'Who?' Sam asked with a suppressed smile, he was not stupid.

'Well, now that you've announced that you're in love with Saira, its really not that important, is it?' I winked, turned around and walked back to the baseline, leaving him wondering for a moment in the middle of the court — known traditionally as no man's land. I had him exactly where I wanted.

What came next was even more ludicrous. Nisha had apparently given Katanga a paper rose. While she had been in the process of stealing him away from his girlfriend, she sat next to him in class one day and sketched a rose on a piece of paper. When the artwork was done, she casually turned around and offered it to Katanga, with a sweet little 'that's for you'. I was astonished when Shiny told me about this; who couldn't see through an obvious, tacky and underhand move like that? Apparently men cannot. You lay it on thick, act as sugary sweet and impossibly cute as you can and the guys will only think you're adorable. The women will see through it and hate you. But the men, they'll love you. Sad, but true.

I couldn't possibly think of an alternative move that matched the paper rose for its sheer stupidity and absurdity, so I decided to just ape it, thinking that this would be the acid test for Nisha's supposedly 'foolproof' modus operandi.

'That's a really good sketch,' Sam commented, seated behind me in the slimy Mrs Sachdeva's maths class. I was almost done so I tore off the page and turned around, saying 'Well, it's for you,' a synthetic saccharine smile plastered across my face, my expression angelic, but feeling totally asinine. I immediately turned around and resumed interest in the class. But not before I had the opportunity to register Sam's stunned, overwhelmed and utterly floored expression. I was halfway home and I couldn't believe it. What was wrong with these boys?

'Don't take it so seriously,' Nisha would tell me when I complained about having to do the bimbo routine. 'Men are just stupid, so play along. Now, it's time to make him jealous.'

I was almost losing interest by then – it was just so disappointing that women were doomed to be sexually attracted to as pathetic a species as men. Why couldn't we date some other creature that wasn't quite so shallow? I empathised with lesbians but unfortunately that wasn't an option for me and I did want to finish the project.

So I roped in my poor old cousin Kartik for a con job. He was not thrilled about it at the outset, but the mention of a Christmas party at The British Embassy School got him to change his mind. For regular school kids in Delhi back then, being invited to an embassy school party was akin to Cinderella being summoned to the royal ball. There were quite a few curious glances and questioning looks as I waltzed in with this good-looking stranger. Kartik and I danced, pretending to be in our own world, all the while laughing under our breaths.

'Look at all these *goris* here,' he whispered to me through clenched teeth. 'And I'm dancing with my sister. This is what hell must be like.'

But dear old Kartik kept an eye on Sam and Saira for me, and according to his reports, Sam kept an eye on us.

Sam was especially chatty with me the next day at school. It was blatantly obvious he was itching to ask. At first he tried to make innocuous conversation, talking about the previous day's astonishing developments on the cricket pitch – Umpire Darrell Hair had no-balled Sri Lankan off-spinner Muttiah Muralitharan an incredible seven times in three overs in a Test against Australia. Even I had started watching a bit of cricket by then – when in Rome, you see. And this was sensational news, but Sam eventually got around to asking what he was trying to get at, attempting to sound nonchalant but failing.

'By the way, are you seeing that guy you came with last night? How come you didn't introduce us?'

'Oh, I would have, but you and Saira looked so caught up in each other, I didn't want to disturb you,' I said, smiling impishly at him, not without a trace of sarcasm in my voice. 'And that guy, he's my brother. Why, what did you think?'

Sam only smiled. And I knew instinctively that I had hit the nail on the head.

By now it was plainly obvious to everyone, including Saira, that Sam had the hots for me. Wagers were on among the crueller population of the school as to when she would be dropped like a hot potato. But Sam didn't make a move. So now, I was to cold-shoulder him. Nisha told me succinctly, 'Lose interest.' It wasn't the same as playing hard to get – that trick she said was ancient, obtuse and hopelessly ineffective. The objective was to exhibit a vague lack of interest. Too many men, too little time – that sorts. And therefore the more Sam's interest seemed to grow, the more I pretended to cool off. I would talk flirty with him at times, but by and large I spent more time talking to other boys in the class, making a big deal of how demanding my social life was, and generally appearing busy, buzzing and preoccupied.

As luck would have it, Sam couldn't have kept me out of his mind even if he tried, because I also became the school heroine that January. As I too would learn later in life, it was one thing to have a crush, but another reality altogether to have a *celebrity* crush.

A cold, foggy Friday morning signalled the last day of Sports Week. It had already been a terrific week for me. I had four medals in the bag – Gold from the cross-country race held on Monday, Silver for the 800m race and for tennis which had concluded just the day before. Another Gold was for the 4 x 400 relay run that same morning. But it was this one I wanted desperately – the 1500m. I had been preparing like a lunatic for it, running twice a day on some days, weights strapped to my ankles, training with the boys' athletics team on a daily basis.

Redhead Lucy Gorzynski stood on my left, dwarfing me by an entire foot at 6'1". Anna Bakhvalova with the crew cut, towered to my right, a leather-studded band on her wrist and a sneer writ large across her face. I had beaten her sister under controversial circumstances to win the 10km cross-country run and it was clear what the junior wanted. I ignored the butterflies in my tummy. The gun went off and instantly the world was shut out. All I saw was the track and the only sound I heard was that of my own breath.

Lucy, Anna and I formed a breakaway group early in the first lap itself. We knew the others were no competition, but who would assert the next push? No one wanted to exert more than was necessary just yet. It was a game of cat and mouse. Halfway through lap two Lucy forced the pace to quicken and Anna and I immediately caught up. We were running on full now. By the third lap Anna was unmistakably beginning to tire – she was breathing heavily and needed effort to keep up with us. Recognising it, Lucy and I pushed harder and began a full-blown sprint. We lost Anna in a matter of seconds. As we entered the last lap, I had a moment of revelation – it was like a voice talking inside my head.

'You're not giving a hundred percent. You can go faster.'

Can I? I thought. Only one way to find out. And I pushed. The machine effortlessly shifted into sixth gear and I rocketed ahead, without feeling the slightest effort. I couldn't believe it even as I ran. Despite my various amorous distractions, the partying, the excesses, the one shred of sanity I had hung onto in the last six months was my training, and it was showing as I gained more and more distance on Lucy. Noises began to filter in. Ms Varma, the PE instructor yelling from the sidelines, 'Go for the record! Go for the school record!' The cheers of my housemates chanting my name. A deafening din as I entered the last stretch and an eruption as I crossed the finish line, a good fifty metres clear of Lucy. I was in a daze. Ms Varma ran up to me, ecstatic, telling me that with my time of 4:44.52. I had just smashed the school record to smithereens! Lucy graciously walked over to congratulate me. My friends Sunil, Mullica and Sudipto ran onto the track and enveloped me in a collective embrace. I saw stars in the daylight.

At the official end of Sports Week I stood on the podium after being named Athlete of the Year with five medals strung happily around my neck. The thunderous applause gave me gooseflesh. It was magic and I was on cloud nine. Sam walked up after the medals ceremony, took my hand under the pretext of congratulating me and virtually sighed 'Congratulations.' I almost felt sorry for him.

Two days later, Sam conveyed the inevitable to Saira and asked me out. It was a wildly triumphant *fait accompli* for Nisha and her protégées. The 10-step guide actually worked; only in my case it had worked in nine and I didn't have to resort to the damsel in distress routine that theoretically concluded the technique. Shiny and I raised a toast of Benadryl Cough Syrup that night, but I didn't feel the elation I might have expected. Sam had not fallen for the real me but for some paper-rose-drawing nitwit. I didn't want a guy who wanted a bimbo.

It did turn out to be a fun-filled relationship with Sam, albeit a short one. In fact it only went kaput because he decided he wanted to marry me and actually tried to get our parents to meet. This being my second successive relationship that disintegrated for much the same reason, I wondered why everybody in India wanted to marry the first person they went out with. Or every person they went out with.

Twelve

To Marry a Cricket Superstar

I was in the clutches of an obsessive, oppressive and suffocating four-year-old relationship. I didn't even know how I had reached such a bleak *cul de sac*. Somewhere between being a free-spirited school girl and an ambitious young woman fresh out of college, I had let myself get sucked into this murky whirlpool.

I was seeing a budding model named Amit, a chauvinistic tyrant who spent the most part of our four years together trying to change my personality. Before him I had entered and exited a series of disastrous relationships with various jerks, idiots, chauvinists and louts, each of which had ended with the men in question trying to make a domesticated wife out of me. And me, putting on my running shoes.

Amit had been different at least in the beginning with his poise, cleverness and middle-class propriety. But no sooner had he muttered the 'M-word' than he started slipping on the leash too. Slowly, covertly. Had I realised what was happening in time, I would have darted out years earlier. It was the lack of substantial grounds that made me hang onto the shrivelled threads of that defunct liaison, eons beyond when it had stopped working. All the while I told myself that this was probably what growing up was about – that I couldn't just go on being a reckless bohemian all my life, I had to learn to make a long-term relationship work.

But I was miserable. I found myself once again in the city where I had spent much of my childhood, only this time life wasn't so much fun. After graduating from Delhi University, I was in pursuit of an ill-advised career in microbiology. I was sitting behind a microscope, working a boring but lucrative job, listlessly drudging from day to dreary day, wondering how it had all gone so horribly wrong.

But the year 2000 brought with it a promise of renaissance. It had been too much of an exciting year in sport for me not to take notice – Ian Thorpe dazzling at the Sydney Olympics, Tiger Woods winning three majors in one calendar year and a heartbreakingly beautiful Russian 20-year-old named Marat Safin winning the US Open tennis. I realised I had become an armchair sportsman, a breed I had always despised. I also realised I was getting older; the champs were suddenly younger than me.

It was time for me to do something about my meaningless existence, and save the real Tanya from the brink of extinction. In the wee hours of one dreary, muggy Mumbai morning I sat up sipping coffee and talking with my eternal ally, Shiny, who was now studying to be a doctor. It was an insightful conversation, one during which I remembered Steffi Graf's wise words, spoken to me in far-off Shenzhen, light-years ago.

'Always do what makes you happy.'

Sports made me happy. It was suddenly so simple. To be happy I needed to make a career in sports, one way or another. Why hadn't I ever realised this earlier?

'I wish we had hindsight in advance,' I sighed as I grasped that I had wasted enough of my life.

I could not begin a career in competitive sport at 22, I knew that much; when teenagers were winning grand slams, I was over the hill. But there were other avenues. So, even as I fussed over chromatography and DNA fragments during the days, I began to study journalism at St. Xavier's in the evenings, devotedly toiling towards a new occupation as a sports writer.

The new college, new friends and new hope started to breathe life back into my cadaver and I sprouted wings once more. I went out with my new classmates and got a life, minus the boyfriend, often sending Amit into jealous rages. But I was beyond the point of tolerating the tantrums now.

To 'rekindle the romance', in his words, Amit planned a weekend getaway to Pune, a three-hour drive away. He had an audition for a television commercial there and decided we could stretch the stay to three days. I didn't mind – a break from any routine was always welcome. So I packed up and went along. Saturday night, after his audition had apparently gone well, we were lounging about at a trendy sports bar called Pegasus. To me, it was such a waste. I was not *allowed* to drink; Mr Manic was very strict about that. So I sank impassively into my bean bag, checking out the cute guys at the billiards table, wondering which one I would like to run away with, dreaming of sipping a cold beer on a sunny island someday.

Then something caught the corner of my eye. A cricket match was playing on the large screen behind the counter and as is the norm in our country, everybody was engrossed. The one good thing that had come out of this ruinous relationship was my love for cricket. When I had first met Amit, he had been appalled that a sports buff like me didn't know much about India's favourite passion. He spent months educating and turning me into a convert. By now I was positively hooked myself. I looked up to see the score in the India versus Kenya match that was underway, but something else got me first.

I felt it like the onset of a fever, my mouth agape, eyes transfixed. The sound of the commentary got increasingly muffled, as if someone had stuffed my ears with cotton. I even felt a bit dizzy. There was a handsome, broad-shouldered young man striding at a furious pace towards the pitch. I watched hypnotised. My eyes had acquired an in-built zoom lens – no, that was some excellent camera work – I could see every crease around the corners of his startling grey eyes as he frowned in concentration, hair damp from perspiration hanging in loose curls over his forehead, feet and shoulders moving in rhythm, as the ball was delivered at nearly 140 kph. It was like watching art in motion.

'Who is he?' I wanted to ask of Amit, but no sound escaped as my mouth opened and shut like that of a guppy. I had to swallow hard. My heart was pounding like an oversized metal drum being beaten furiously with a hammer.

'This guy is amazing, man!' Amit exclaimed, thumping the table animatedly as the batsman's middle stump went flying and somersaulting into the distance. 'Did you see that?' he turned to me excitedly.

'Who is he?' I finally managed to squeak, careful not to let on the rush of desire that I was feeling for this stranger who was bowling for India.

'His name is Nasir Naqvi,' Amit replied, blissfully unaware of the frenzied activity going on inside my head. 'Don't you know? He's the new guy they picked for this series.'

Oh yes, I had heard that name on the news only a few days back. But there had been no footage; he was virtually an unknown from a small town near Nagpur. Surely there must have been post-selection interviews on all the news channels, but I had missed them somehow. Well, I wasn't going to miss a single one from here on. Obsession swathed me like a landslide, stronger, more intense than anything I had felt before.

I wore my heart on my sleeve. My college file was encased in paraphernalia, from photographs to printouts of domestic and international cricket schedules. I emphatically announced to my journalism class that I was going to marry him. Most indulged me, some ignored me and some like the holier-than-thou Anupriya Verma cautioned me against such wanton behaviour. Most inspiring of all though was Shaila, who would tell me to 'just do it'. Of course, she had a vested interest – should I figure out exactly how to get hitched to Nasir, she was to use the same formula to snare Indian vice-captain, Rahil David. And so we formed a mutual encouragement society and went absolutely bananas planning our futures as superstar wives.

The regular hangout for us those days was a quaint little rooftop café at Colaba Causeway called Cloud Nine. It was almost like the European sidewalk cafés in its warmth, al fresco charm and relaxed air. You could sit there for hours nursing a single coffee, if at all one, and the waiters and manager would only smile. Not to mention the magnificent ninth floor view of the South Mumbai skyline, which was spectacular as it drowned into sunset. Every evening after class, we girls would gather at Cloud Nine for an hour or two to chat, gossip and generally unwind.

One evening, we were forced to sit indoors for a change, thanks to a torrential Mumbai downpour. A recent cricket match was playing on the television monitors inside, but because it was a replay not too many diners were interested. A bunch of young men though, corporate banker types, were on the table adjacent to ours and were enthralled. Just as they collectively applauded one of Nasir's now famous in-swingers, I couldn't help myself.

'I'm going to marry this man,' I stood up and announced, swelling with pride as though a date had been set. 'Say hello to Mrs Nasir Naqvi.' The men looked stunned for a moment, probably wondering who I was talking to, but recovered gamely enough and raised their beer glasses to me in good cheer.

'Well, congratulations!' One of them yelled across the tables. 'Give him our respect, he's awesome.'

'Is he playing in the Ranji match tomorrow at the MIG?' Another one asked.

Huh? Had these fellows taken me seriously? I suppose they had – not too many women would publicly broadcast an engagement that was entirely fictitious.

'Um, yes, he is,' I replied with a wide smile, not entirely sure myself. He did play for Maharashtra and there was, after all, a Mumbai versus Maharashtra match the next day. 'I'll pass on your wishes.'

My friends Naina, Preeti and Shaila slid into fits of giggles as I parked myself back down, feeling extremely silly but thrilled to bits nonetheless. I had a new plan – I was going to go to the MIG stadium and watch that match in person the next day. Surely there would be a chance to meet the players? Gosh, why hadn't I thought of this before? Unfortunately no one in my immediate party was even remotely interested in spending a whole day watching a domestic game, so I called up a colleague from work, who I knew to be a big cricket fan, and begged him to arrange for a couple of tickets.

I hadn't been inside a sports arena to watch live professional sport since my schooldays in Hong Kong, and that, was a lifetime ago. I had forgotten the buzz, the adrenaline rush of being in the stands, swaying with the crowds, applauding and cheering. And my presumption that domestic cricket had few takers was entirely wrong; the Mumbai locals had assembled in droves to support their home grown-heroes with fervour. My colleague Vinay was convinced I was going to get us both lynched – I was the lone voice in the stadium cheering every Mumbai wicket and egging the opposition bowlers on. There he was, the love of my life, Nasir Naqvi, looking every bit the Adonis I had thought he would be. The run-up was faster in life than it seemed on television and the delivery even fiercer. He was also a showman, playing to the galleries and celebrating like a barbaric hunter each time he claimed a scalp. He reminded me of the 1985 Wimbledon champion. I loved every bit of it.

After the day's play was over, I asked Vinay if he wanted to try and get some autographs. He declared it was immature and he wasn't in the least bit interested. I think he was disappointed – he had thought my asking him to come along was some sort of a date. But upon spending the entire day seated next to a madwoman screaming 'I love you Nasir!' he probably felt there hadn't been that much in it for him after all.

There was a regular mob outside the players' dressing rooms, largely made up of adolescents and children. I felt like Old Mother Hubbard. Undeterred, I made my way to the front of the throbbing mass, thinking nothing of elbowing eight-year-olds out of my way. If only they had known who they were standing next to – the future Mrs Naqvi – they might have shown some respect and voluntarily parted like the Red Sea.

Ajay Avishkar suddenly appeared at the door and weaved his way through, stopping to sign a couple of autographs en route. I wondered if it would be too discourteous to ask him when Nasir might be stepping out and decided against it. Next came Jatin Talwarkar and instantly, like moths to a flame, the entire swarm of human beings flitted across and swathed him. Now this was one autograph that would actually be valuable, but just as I was considering fighting the masses to get one, my hero appeared at the doorway like a divine apparition. Nasir Naqvi, in the flesh and blood, stood just two metres away from me. My heart simply surrendered and stopped beating. He was breathtaking. He was also eyeing the crowd apprehensively, looking extremely uncomfortable and awkward. 'Poor baby isn't quite used to this adulation yet,' I thought to myself.

I rushed to him.

'Autograph please,' beaming, I looked up at him, towering almost a foot and a half above me. He looked down, puzzled.

'On that?' he said, raising his eyebrows. He actually spoke to me! I couldn't believe it – I was talking to Nasir Naqvi. But why did I feel a tad disappointed? Perhaps it was the unanticipated squeaky voice. I had been expecting a reverberating baritone. Never mind. What had he said? I glanced down to see the bright yellow envelope that I had hastily rummaged from my purse and thrust at him. A few little boys had meanwhile collected around me, and were impatiently waiting their turn.

'Yes please,' I attempted to generate the sweetest smile ever. Without further ado, Nasir robotically signed my yellow envelope.

Needless to say, the autograph looked like nothing. Not even a close relative of the Roman script. Why was he being so stuffy about signing on an envelope? What had he expected from a 23-year-old? A dainty little autograph book, with teddy bears at the corners?

'Can I take a photograph with you please?' I whipped out my little digital before Nasir could have a moment to register my request, quickly handed it to the oldest looking adolescent bystander and happily posed for the snap. My fellow autograph-seeker gladly obliged and took the picture, grinning from ear to ear, baring his braces. I felt on top of the world. I could have kissed him right there – Nasir, not the pre-teen.

After signing another couple of obligatory autographs, Nasir manoeuvred past the crowd and managed to squeeze into the elevator just as the doors were shutting. Not wanting to waste even those last few precious seconds, I coquettishly flashed a couple of 'come hither' glances at Nasir through mascara-ed lashes. He registered the vibes and for a moment there I thought he was staring right back at me.

Apparently not. Nasir had sleepwalked through the entire exercise, as was evident once I checked out the photos. It was such a disappointment – not only did he look half-asleep and totally uninterested in the picture, but I looked like a fat cow! I didn't think I was fat, hadn't been since I was eleven, but the picture told me otherwise. Standing next to a 6'4" professional athlete, I looked like a tomato wearing a tight belt. Clearly, I had let myself go. I wallowed in depression for the following few days thinking 'I'm too fat; I'll never get him looking like this. Superstars go out with models and actresses, not with roly-poly fans.'

Fuelled by inspiration and love, I furiously launched into a total makeover campaign. I began walking the five miles to and from college daily, signed up for morning tennis at the local club, lost ten pounds, gained a new wardrobe, got highlights and a sassy new haircut. It worked.

A couple of months into my metamorphosis, I announced with renewed confidence that it was time for strike two. India was playing a One Day International against the West Indies in Pune that coming weekend and there, I decided, the two star-crossed lovers shall meet again. The supporting cast would be my Xavier friends – Naina, Preeti, Shaila and Pranav. Shaila's film-producer father conveniently maintained an apartment in one of Pune's hippest districts, while Pranav's girlfriend Tanaz – who was also coming along – had her own villa in the college capital. So basically, we were spoilt for choice as far as a roof over our heads was concerned. Not that we planned to spend much time indoors; well, Pranav and Tanaz sure did, but the rest of us were off to the rundown little stadium before we'd had time to unpack.

It was that electric atmosphere all over again; only this time it was an international match, so multiply that to the power of infinity. The public was going crazy, and news channels buzzed about with their omnipresent OB vans and general hysteria saturated the stadium. Our little gang of girls was armed for a regular trophy hunt – hats and dark glasses, red lipstick, deep-necked sundresses, binoculars and 5-inch stilettos. Surely there would have been more than a few casualties, but who was counting? Our eyes were fixed, mostly through the binoculars, on the No. 33 shirt fielding at the boundary.

'Why are we all watching your lover boy?' laughed Preeti, who singularly made it possible for a human being to look exactly like a cuddly teddy bear.

'Coz he's just so hot,' I sniggered and snatched the binoculars right back from her.

India lost the match and while a pall of gloom hung through most of the stadium, I was smiling like the cat that got the cream. I had, after all, spent the entire eight or so hours ogling my darling. Heck, through the binoculars, it felt like I had indulged in an intimate conversation with him the whole day. Who cared who won the match?

That night, we assumed the player's party – we had heard of such events – would take place at Scream, the nightclub at the official team hotel. Sure enough, we trooped in *en masse*, coughing up hitherto unheard of sums for the entry. We got to party with the cricketers all right, but unfortunately for me, it was the wrong team. The world's second-best batsman was lounging about at the bar, chatting with a bevy of models. A few of his team-mates were burning up the dance floor the way only Caribbean men can. The atmosphere was heady and you would think I would have made the most of the chance to hang out with some of the biggest names in world cricket. But nope, all I could do was mope and wonder why the Indian team were such nerds that they couldn't even hop down for a little shimmying?

A few familiar Indian faces were in attendance though. Visages from the past; former captains and match winners who were today's commentators and television experts, bespectacled and paunchy, I might add. But one look at some of them and you'd think they were experiencing the first flush of youth – raunchy dances with girls half their age, drunken smirks perfecting the look.

We got Pranav, the sweetheart that he was, to do the dirty work.

'Err, excuse me,' he awkwardly interrupted a particularly inebriated former Indian captain. 'Is there any chance of seeing the Indian cricketers here tonight?'

'Which Indian cricketers? We are Indian cricketers,' the aging superstar said gruffly, irritated at having been intruded upon halfway through a John Travolta-like dance move.

As soon as Pranav pointed at us and said the magic words, 'I think those girls over there want to know about the current team,' the brusque manner flipped instantly and he flashed a cheesy moustached smile in our direction. 'Hey girls!' he slurred at us, grinning uncontrollably while the rest of his contemporaries leered on. 'Cricketers are like wine, we only get better with age.'

What a creep. The only consolation was that Pranav actually muttered, 'Aren't you married, old man?' before walking off from that bizarre bunch. Apparently, cricketers don't party after losing a match. That was a thumb rule I would learn later. But for that evening, we had to make do with old fogies and each other.

Everything changed from the day the South African cricket team arrived in India for what would eventually be a historic tour. The imminent 3-Test series against the world beaters generated a great deal of anticipation, and cricket fever was virtually an epidemic in the nation. To celebrate the start of the tour, and to formally welcome the visiting team, the Cricket Club of India hosted a spectacular charity dinner and celebrity match on a beautiful February evening. As you can imagine, the competition for passes and tickets was murderous, but fortunately for me, my parents were CCI members and had first right to purchase tickets.

It was a magical soiree at the illuminated Brabourne Stadium. Faces one normally saw on magazine covers and newsstands strolled around nonchalantly, hackles down for a change. Film stars, politicians, tennis champions and of course, cricketers past and present. The two teams that were to take each other on in the exhibition match were assorted, comprising a combination of old and young sportsmen as well as enthusiastic matinee idols. The main pavilion was overflowing with celebrities the way a popular London pub might on a Saturday night, and the security guards weren't making too much of a fuss about autograph hunters. Shiny made a beeline for the film stars; I naturally, turned to the cricketers. But I stopped short of actually asking for autographs. Because right there, ten feet away from me across the fence, sat the object of my obsession. And I had correctly decided that my previous behaviour at the MIG Club had been a fiasco. I couldn't just be another face in the crowd, a mere fan. No, I had to treat him as though he was mortal, not divine.

And so I stared. Simply and shamelessly. If ever there was a beckoning gaze on the face of this planet, it was at the Brabourne Stadium that evening, emanating from a girl in a red dress, directed at a magnificent young man who sat on the steps of the pavilion. I sent such strong vibes; you could almost reach out and pluck them like forbidden apples. Nasir turned around and saw me trying to magnetise him from outside the fence, and looked away. He changed position, and moved behind a pillar to get out of my line of sight. I felt like the Big Bad Wolf. Promptly, I moved along the fence, (the better to see you with My Dear). It was such fun. I was smirking now, enjoying this game. He was just a guy after all. And moreover, what did I have to lose?

Suddenly he got up and started walking straight towards me. Uh oh. This wasn't in my script. Utterly flustered, I didn't know what to do. The self-assured seductress was gone in the blink of an eye. I just wanted to run. Mercifully, Shiny walked back to me just in the nick of time.

'He's coming here!' I yelled and whispered simultaneously, grabbing hold of her arm. 'Do something.'

'What? Who's coming?' Poor Shiny had no clue what planet I was on. She was trying to show me an Aamir Khan autograph that she had just managed to get. 'What's wrong?'

'Shiny, shut up and listen to me. Nasir is coming here – to me, to us. You have to ask him for an autograph or something because I don't know what to say.'

'Huh?' was all Shiny could manage before she turned around to see that Nasir was, indeed, walking straight to us, a bemused smile upon his face. I thought I was going to die.

'Hi!' Good old Shiny said as normally as was humanly possible in that bizarre situation. 'I'm a big fan; can I have your autograph please?'

I just stood there beside her, pretending to be a waxwork statue, absolutely mortified. Nasir calmly signed Shiny's notepad, looking at me all the while, smiling as if there were some private joke between the two of us. I couldn't believe it – he was turning the tables on me!

'I think I've seen you somewhere,' he said, his eyes boring right through to my heart, making me feel faint. He knew it too and was unmistakably enjoying it. He's talking to me, I thought to myself. He's trying to have a conversation with me, even though I didn't ask for the autograph. Quick, idiot, say something.

'Probably you have. I'm studying to be a sports journalist so I attend almost every match possible. You must have seen me in the stands somewhere.'

And I walked off.

I actually walked off.

Shiny and Nasir were left standing there, smiling politely at each other.

Outside, in the car park, I pulled out my cell phone to call Preeti, my fingers trembling. My heart was beating so fast, I thought it would explode.

'Are you crazy, woman?' was all Preeti could say by the time I explained to her what had just transpired. '*I think I've seen you somewhere* is a pick-up line, you ass. The guy of your dreams just dropped you a pick-up line and you walked off? You should be shot.'

She was right. I really did want to shoot myself. Why did I do that? And as if right on cue, Shiny found me and asked me the same thing. 'Da, why on earth did you just do that?' I had no answer. I couldn't explain it even to myself. All I knew was that if I had continued standing there, trying to hold a conversation with him, I would have either choked to death or peed in my pants. Neither would have been a charming move.

Would I regret that moment forever after?

Not if I could help it. I had been struck dumb once, but I was certainly not the kind to give up after one foiled operation. I was going to get Nasir after all. The first Test match between India and South Africa was due to start in Mumbai within a few days, and I made sure Papa arranged for VIP box seats through the CCI for all five days. With fresh gusto, I hauled Naina along, who didn't know the ABC of cricket, and marched off to the grand Wankhede.

Needless to say, I hardly watched the game; I watched only him, through my father's by-now grossly misused binoculars. Not that I missed very much; the mauling the Indian bowlers received that day at the hands of the dashing opening pair bordered on comical. By the end of the first day's play, the match looked like it would be over and done in three days flat. As the disappointed spectators filed out of the stadium, I lingered on, hoping to catch another glimpse of my man. Players of both sides were now scattered about on the field, towelling off, stretching and cooling down. I begged Naina to remain a little longer with me in the empty stands – we were after all, in the VIP box, it wasn't as if someone would try to shunt us out – and she agreed, amused as always with my puerile behaviour. Undoubtedly, my obsession was a great source of entertainment to all my friends. But then out of the blue, Nasir gave Naina good enough reason to stop chuckling at me. He was looking right at us. Nasir was watching me! He was touching his toes, but looking at me. Seated on the ground, a good fifty yards away from us, with his back to the rest of his squad, staring at me! And then he waved. My heart stopped beating.

'Wave back!' Even the mild-mannered Naina snapped at my inconstant.

'Is he really waving at me?' I asked, knowing fully well that he was, but my mind refusing to believe it.

'Yes! Wave back, NOW!'

And so I did. But it was too late; he had already turned around and rejoined his team-mates. I couldn't believe it – this was the second opportunity that I had completely bungled. How would I ever forgive myself?

I held a very solemn conversation with Naina, Preeti and Shaila over dinner at the Radio Club that evening.

'Do you think I'm doing this on purpose? I mean, maybe my subconscious doesn't want this to happen or something. Maybe, it's just convenient to have him out of reach, for him to be unattainable.'

'But why?' Naina, always the sensible one, asked. 'Clearly, he has shown some interest. Why would you not want this to work out?'

'Maybe I'm terrified of Amit,' I sighed, knowing all too well that this was what had been eating me all along. 'And I feel guilty.

Don't forget, I do have a boyfriend who's away in Seychelles shooting for a TV series right now. But he will be back one day and maybe that's just the reality of my life. Maybe this whole Nasir fantasy is meant to be just that – a fantasy.'

'Well then, you need to see it that way and not get so involved,' Naina offered, trying to be helpful. 'You don't want to ruin a four-year relationship over a celebrity crush do you?'

'Naina this is not a joke anymore,' I wailed, on the verge of tears. 'He spoke to me, waved to me, you saw it. I feel like I could have made something of it. It doesn't feel like a dream anymore, it feels like it could have happened. And why stay in a relationship that makes me miserable?'

Preeti agreed wholeheartedly. 'Absolutely, whether this thing with Nasir happens or not, it's really obvious that you need to get out of your current relationship. You wouldn't be pining for another man so desperately if you really were in love with Amit.'

I silently nodded in accordance. I had known this for a long time now, just not acted upon it. I had been on the verge of breaking up several times, but had never taken the final step. A few other romantic interests had flickered over the years, but never one strong enough to shake me out of my passive stupor. Nasir was different – this one had hit me like a tornado. I couldn't *not* take this chance.

'And anyway, I don't see why you're giving up,' Shaila said, perking up. 'If I was in your place, I'd be encouraged. You'll get more opportunities to meet him; just don't act like a zombie next time. After all, even cricketers are just men, right? They do basically end up with women. And you're a woman. Get it?'

I loved Shaila.

India did go onto lose the first Test match miserably in the space of three days. I was drowning in despondency not because India lost, but because the teams would now have to travel to the next venue, another city. I was running out of time, I had to do something quick. The brilliant plan I came up with was to lounge about in the lobby of the Oberoi Sheraton Towers at Nariman Point – I had heard this was where the teams had been put up. Preeti and Naina gamely tagged along. It was a glorious wasted afternoon. Not everyday did college students sip expensive coffee in fine-china served in the sunny lobby of a luxurious 7-star hotel. No cricketers in sight, but we enjoyed ourselves, laughing at the inanity of the situation.

'Is this what groupies do?' Naina asked, giggling. She was dressed plainly as always, but a smile always lit up her personality.

'No, groupies get more lucky,' I retorted and we all laughed.

Back at my house that evening, Preeti – who was staying over – decided to give her sister's fiancé a call. He was in the hotel business and we thought asking him to do a little sleuthing for us wouldn't hurt. It was the best idea we'd had all day. Turned out, the cricketers were staying at the Juhu Centaur, a galaxy away from Nariman Point and were due to check out early next morning.

'Now what?' I inquired. 'It's a little late in the day to go all the way to Juhu.' This was Mumbai, after all, where people avoided travelling from town to the suburbs unless their life depended on it, and even then, just maybe.

'Let's try to call,' came Preeti's ingenuous suggestion.

'Do you think it's going to be that easy? We just call up and ask for him?'

'Well, there's no harm in trying.'

She had a point. Immediately, we got down to business; looked up the hotel's numbers in the directory and put a call through, all fingers crossed. I asked the receptionist to connect me to Nasir Naqvi in a calm voice, belying my nerves. She informed me he wasn't staying at their hotel. Obviously. As if they would put just anyone's call through.

'Let's call again and ask for another player,' Preeti proposed, never one to give up easily. 'Maybe he's really not checked in, but some others are.'

I thought about it for a moment. Nasir was known to be great pals with Karan Rathore. Maybe if we could get through to him . . . .

'Connect me to Karan Rathore please,' Preeti demanded in a polite, firm and surprisingly sounded mature and older.

'May I have the room number, ma'am?' I could hear the robotic voice of the receptionist at the other end.

'Don't be silly, *bachhe*, I'm his mother,' Preeti said with such authority that I had to cover my mouth to suppress a guffaw. No way was this going to work.

Connected! They were putting us through to a room. We couldn't believe it. Preeti, perched precariously on my dresser until then, nearly fell off in excitement. Someone came on the line.

'Okay, who is this?' A deep, sexy voice with a pleasant, amiable quality. 'Because I know it's not my mother.'

I had to laugh out loud. Preeti apologised to him, saying she hadn't meant to bother him and that he was a great player and all that, but could he please tell her Nasir's room number.

'Who are you?' Karan asked, a smile in his voice.

'Who am I?' Preeti urgently whispered and gestured to me, at a loss for what to say. I scratched my head. '*Bhabhi*!' I shot back. 'Say you're his *bhabhi* and try to sound a bit vernacular.'

'I'm his *bhabhi*,' she said, her accent suddenly like that of someone who had graduated from the Happy Marathi School or some such entity. I exploded with laughter, causing Preeti to do pretty much the same.

'If you're his *bhabhi*, shouldn't you know that he is not checked into the hotel because he lives in Mumbai?' Karan ragged her, clearly enjoying this charade as much as we were. Bloody hell! Nasir lived in Mumbai? But good old Karan apparently had a great sense of humour, or an immense talent for chasing skirts.

'But since you are his *bhabhi* and want to talk to him, I'll give you his cell number.'

Oh. My. God. This could not be happening. I started jumping up and down, my synapses were shooting off in all directions. Preeti snatched a pen and jotted down the number on a very sweaty palm. Once she had hung up, we stared at each other for a few moments. This was it. I had Nasir's cell number. With a long breath of air, I mustered up the nerve to call.

'Hullo?' The voice I would come to recognise so well.

'Hi Nasir,' I said softly, blood rushing from my head to my toes, heart pounding to some senseless rhythm. 'I'm a big fan of yours and first of all I want to say I'm sorry; I got your number by telling Karan Rathore that I'm your *bhabhi*. It's just that I really wanted to talk to you and wish you all the best for the next match and for your entire future . . . . '

'Are you? . . . Aren't you the girl who was in the stadium today, wearing the white shirt and blue jeans? You were dancing like crazy every time I took a wicket,' he laughed.

Wait a second. What? This is insane. This is ridiculous. How could he know that?

'Huh?' was all I managed to say. 'H-h-how do you know?'

'I saw you today, in fact, everyday over the past three days.'

Hello people, this was Nasir Naqvi speaking to me. I was too numb to react.

He continued. 'You're the same girl I met at that dinner at CCI, aren't you? I remember you told me that you are always at every match, and since then I always look for you in the stands. Whenever I am fielding at the boundary or waiting in the pavilion, I search the faces for you.'

Excuse me? Would someone please pinch me and wake me up? This was too good to be true. This was ludicrous.

'Why?' I was barely able to generate the word.

'You won't believe this, but when I went home after that night at CCI I felt as if I know you and I was sure we're going to meet again. I even told my brother about you,' Nasir said, slowly, warily. 'And just now, when you called, you had just said hello and I knew it was you. Don't ask me how, I just did.'

'I don't know what to say.' But I wanted to turn cartwheels. How on earth was this possible, among hundreds of thousands of adoring fans, through a maze of millions of faces in the stadiums, how had he zeroed in on me like I had zeroed in on him? This was fate. There was simply no other explanation. The higher powers of the universe had decided we were meant to be together.

The next 24 hours went by in a blur, like a drunken stupor. We couldn't hang up. We tried it a few times and then just gave up and went on talking about him, me, us, life, the sky, the earth. My maid brought my dinner to my room only to find my lunch tray untouched from six hours ago. I couldn't eat, I couldn't sleep. All those clichés that Hindi movies propagate about love were extraordinarily coming true. Shiny knew what was going on, and aside from barely being able to believe it, was most amused at my condition.

Over the course of the conversation it also came up that I reminded him of his high school crush.

'You know, you look exactly like the girl I used to be in love with when I was in school,' he said. 'She never gave me the time of day, didn't even look at me once.'

'Oh, how she must be regretting that now!' I laughed. 'Wait a minute, is that the reason you got interested in me?'

'Well, at first, maybe,' he said. 'I even remember you took my autograph after that Ranji game at the MIG. But you're different. . . .'

'Oh no!' I exclaimed, interrupting him. 'I had hoped you wouldn't remember *that* meeting. I was a fat cow.' Apparently, he had *not* sleepwalked through that episode and *had* noticed the tomato wearing a belt after all.

'No, you weren't,' he chuckled back. 'You were cute and funny, fighting with all those kids to get my autograph. I thought you were beautiful. And now that I'm talking to you, you're not like her at all. She was introverted and arrogant. You're always laughing and talking and saying exactly what's on your mind. I think you're adorable.'

I did a little silent jig right there in my room. We talked on the phone non-stop till ten the next morning, when he had no choice but to leave for the airport. The team had important business to take care of, like salvaging the series. But that's how things progressed for us – everyday we would talk on the phone for hours, after he had finished with practice or on certain days, after an actual match. I got first-hand accounts of India's miraculous Test match win in Kolkata where Rahil David and S. Ram put up a superhuman effort and then, euphoric details of the series victory in Bengalooru, brought about by the Turbaned Wonder. Those were magical times; we were very much in love and India was winning again.

'Do you know what my mobile bill is for this last month?' Nasir laughed as we talked the day after their historic win. 'Only rupees 94,000.'

I burst out laughing, part guilt, part smugness. 'It's okay. You of all people can afford it, Mr Superstar.'

He hated it when I addressed him that way. Such talk was taboo territory.

'I'm going to frame this bill and put it up in our house after we get married,' he chuckled.

Married?

Nasir had spoken as though it was understood. For the first time in my life my heart jumped with joy upon hearing those words. I had spent my entire adult romantic life playing the runaway bride-to-be. Deep in my heart I had believed marriage simply wasn't something I was cut out for. It was as if I was missing a gene or something. Even with Amit, a regular source of discord between us had been my absolute refusal to commit to any sort of lifelong contract, even after four years together. This one had been a measly two months, but I was ecstatic.

But I decided not to let on just how thrilled I was, so I casually changed the topic.

'When are we finally going to meet?' I implored. We had still not met since the fateful day I had called him. With his national duties now over for the time being, we were looking forward to throwing ourselves in each other's arms.

'You know, I think it's been for the best,' he said. 'We got to know each other so well on the phone, without meeting face to face and possibly getting carried away by physical attraction.'

I was touched. Especially after being used to the despot I had recently broken up with. What a mature and sensible observation, I thought to myself. Not bad for a man! And that too, for an Indian man from a small town. Maybe I would marry him after all.

'He wants to marry you?' Preeti screamed when I told her. 'But he hasn't even gone to college! What will you both talk about?'

I laughed and told her with a body like his, who needed conversation? My mother's take on the issue was entirely different though. When Shiny gingerly informed her that a member of the Indian cricket team wanted to marry her elder daughter, Mum immediately knew who we were referring to. Much as we'd like to believe otherwise, parents always know exactly what's going on.

'Over my dead body,' came the composed, unruffled reply.

'But why not?' Shiny inquired. I too, had sneaked out of my bedroom by now, to try and gauge the direction their discussion was taking. Apparently, it had hit a brick wall.

'Because if my daughter tries to marry a Muslim, I'll either jump off the balcony or throw her off it. Your poor dead grandfather will turn in his grave,' she shuddered.

And that was it.

Finally, Nasir and I met and it was better than we had dared to imagine. We got along with such an easy camaraderie that the gulf between our backgrounds and education seemed inconsequential, at least at first. He possessed a childlike sense of humour that kept me in splits, as well as a disarming humility that struck the right chords. And the chemistry? The test tube runneth over.

It soon blossomed into a wonderful symbiotic relationship where I would familiarise him with the finer side of life – designer labels, Japanese cuisine, a better vocabulary – and he would provide me with the joys only the girlfriend of a celebrity can experience like always being ushered to the best table in the house, getting the 'inside stuff' from the Indian dressing room and generally being the cynosure of all eyes. It was enough to make me giddy to the bone.

The day came when Nasir wanted me to meet his family. It was a big step for him. Up until then, he had never even had a friend that was a girl, let alone a girlfriend. Of course, there had been several brief encounters with the authentic groupie-types, mandatory for a demigod of his stature, but those were liaisons his family obviously didn't know about. He informed his family that he was bringing a female friend along to help pick the outfits for his brother's upcoming wedding. Assuming that was all he had divulged yet to his orthodox clan, I confidently and cheerfully strode into the D&G showroom, where I had asked them to meet me. Taking me completely by surprise, Nasir coolly introduced me to his brothers, including the groom-to-be, as '*tumhari bhabhi*'. I was stunned.

I glared up at him with a look that said, 'You should have warned me.' I would have at least worn a *salwar kameez*. He only seemed confused and disappointed that I didn't beam at the introduction.

Thankfully, the remainder of the rendezvous progressed pretty well, if you discount his mother's less-than-affectionate glances in my direction. The brothers and the father seemed to have taken to me well and were sweet, gracious and indulgent. I enthusiastically began to pick out a few men's suits, but was stopped short by Mother Dear who crustily announced to no one in particular that this shop was outrageously expensive and beyond their means. Beyond their means? Lady, what are you talking about, I felt like hollering, do you even know how much money your son makes? Evidently, she had not yet come to terms with her son's evolving lifestyle and financial status. I felt stupid and incongruous, and hoped that my sincere effort to please hadn't come across as condescending or snobbish.

'Don't worry mother, we're rich now,' a tasteful statement to that effect from his brother, came to my rescue.

And so the suits were finalised, although I was not too ecstatic about Nasir's choice of dark green for himself. I had been leaning more towards the camel or the taupe. As we were saying goodbye, I whispered to him.

'Don't you think you should have told me you were going to introduce me as your girlfriend? I would have worn something more appropriate. Your mom clearly doesn't like me very much.'

'No, I'm glad you met her in your jeans and T-shirt,' he replied with that disarming smile. 'They should get to know you as you really are.'

Man, this guy meant business. And I was glad to note that he possessed a certain natural urbanity and open mindedness that was in stark contrast to his socio-economic background. But then he jolted me out of my reverie with the most insane question ever.

'But, she will want you to convert. You will convert, won't you?'

Convert?

'Convert what?' I asked, too shocked to even be sure of what he was getting at.

'Your religion. You will come into my religion, won't you?'

I couldn't believe it. How could anyone impose such an enormous obligation on another human being? Why should I convert? Why should anyone? Some gall he had.

'Of course not,' was my curt response and we left it at that.

I was so peeved after this little interface that I went home and seriously thought about where this relationship was heading. But then I reconsidered the fact that he was also the sweetest guy I had ever known. He was fun, attentive, composed and on the bloody

Indian cricket team, so I decided to continue having a blast and falling harder in love.

Meanwhile, my professional life was at the crossroads and I was finally ready to embark upon an entirely new direction. After having completed my journalism studies, I had landed a promising job as a sports reporter with *the Hindustan*, one of the largest circulating national dailies. During my interview I had convinced the dapper Jaiveer Singhvi, then editor of the *Hindustan*, to recruit me for his sports desk. I told him I'd rather be a coffee girl on the sports desk than editor of HT City. He bought my argument with a healthy dose of humour and my appointment letter was handed to me. Only hitch was that the job was in Delhi. There had been a few offers from local Mumbai newspapers as well, but none as juicy as this one. I couldn't possibly pass up the chance – this would hurl me directly into the big league.

Nasir tried in vain to stop me from moving, but the four years in jail with Amit had taught me that I was never again going to compromise my freedom for a man. My new career, my dreams and my identity would always come first no matter what – I had made that promise to myself. And I truly believed that if the relationship had to work, it would anyway. Reluctantly, Nasir agreed to keep the fires burning long distance. He would make as many stopovers in Delhi as possible, while I would run off to Mumbai at the slightest opportunity.

'Are you seeing anyone?' my cousin Saurav asked, as we drove from the airport to his house in Delhi, always my favourite place in the world. We hadn't met in a while and there was quite a bit of catching up to do. He knew I was not seeing Amit anymore – and like the rest of my family was incredibly thankful for it – but he was not aware of my latest affair.

'Yup, his name's Nasir,' I said, suppressing a smile.

'Okay,' Saurav replied carefully. My family being an endearing assortment of bigots and fanatics, it took great character for him not to have a knee-jerk reaction to the ethnicity of the name. 'What does he do?'

'He plays cricket for India.'

Saurav coughed so hard and slammed on the brakes so fast that we nearly swerved into a cow's rump. I burst out into a guffaw and he turned to me with an incredulous grin plastered all over his face.

'Okay,' he nodded, and didn't restart the car or say anything else until a good five minutes later.

That was mostly the reaction I got from my extended family, most of whom were thrilled to have a cricket superstar in their midst. All my younger cousins would line up to have a word with him on the phone every time he called from far-off lands like Bulawayo or Johannesburg. Needless to say, I didn't divulge my little joyful secret to anyone and everyone, and certainly not my new colleagues in the media. They would have had me for supper – I was learning what a cutthroat world journalism was.

And so the romance continued. I routinely sneaked off to Mumbai for weekends and often even travelled abroad with him, secretly of course, to avoid the attention of my fellow hacks. But the poor Indian team's media manager was forever perplexed as he discovered me dining with the boys in one of the players' rooms or hanging around in the hotel casino with them. He believed I was disregarding all protocol by forcing my way to unauthorised interviews and would promptly escort me out, only to find me lounging in the pool deck half an hour later with Nasir and Karan. It was a laugh riot.

And it was also a rare opportunity to get to know some of the most elusive folks in the country, on a personal level. They were such a fabulous bunch of boys, most of them from humble backgrounds who had been thrust into the glaring spotlight. And it was only with each other that they let their hair down – quite literally in the case of the Turbaned Wonder. I was witness to precious moments like a drunk Jatin Talwarkar playing golf in the corridors of a hotel in Sri Lanka, or watching Sanjay Leela Bhansali's super bore *Devdas* with half the Indian squad at a theatre in Central London.

The undisputed highlight of this privileged access came when Nasir first introduced me to his captain, Gaurav Mukherjee. The two of us were sharing a quiet dinner at the team hotel upon the squad's return from Zimbabwe, when I noticed Gaurav walking towards us.

'Oh I told him about you,' Nasir informed me, wiping his mouth with the napkin. 'He wants to meet you.'

Thrilled, I stood up to greet the captain of the Indian cricket team, but before I could say a word, Gaurav stretched out his arm to offer a handshake and said, 'Hi, my name is Gaurav, nice to meet you.'

I wobbled on my feet. You don't have to tell me your name, I felt like shouting. The whole world knows who you are! After I had clumsily introduced myself, Gaurav pulled my chair further out for me, so I could sit back down without toppling over. Such manners. By the end of the evening, I was totally swept off my feet. Not only was he courteous, witty and sophisticated, but also amiable and unassuming – virtues the press never gave him credit for.

Life had never been more fun, but perhaps because I was enjoying myself too much with the business of living it, I failed to pay heed when the cracks began to appear. My move to Delhi was beginning to bother Nasir, I could tell, but I didn't attempt to do a thing about it. He never said anything, but his voice often became strained. Whispers about him philandering also began to find their way to me but each time I questioned him, he scoffed at the rumours and I was happy to believe him.

'Are you really going to marry him next year?' asked Naina, who was now not only a friend and fellow journalist, but also living with me in my grandfather's old bungalow in Hauz Khas.

'I don't really know if I want to marry him just yet,' I said, but inside I felt myself smiling and thinking: I will; why the hell not?

It was late September and the air had begun to acquire the crisp scent that would envelop the city through the coming season – a beautiful five months during which New Delhi blossomed. I hadn't heard from Nasir in days, but I accounted it to the fact that he was undeniably busy with his brother's wedding. Nasir had said I wouldn't be able to deal with an orthodox Muslim wedding in a squalid small town, and I had accepted that statement at face value. So I didn't attend the wedding and waited for him to call. But he didn't. Little warning bells began to go off in my head – he had never gone 24 hours without calling me. What was happening?

Finally when he did call, I knew instantly from the tone of his voice that something was terribly wrong. He tried to make a standard conversation, apologised for not having been in touch, but he sounded edgy.

'Nasir, please tell me what is wrong,' I said, a foreboding cloaking me like a shadow. 'I know something's not right, you've been so . . . distant . . .'

A long sigh at the other end of the line. And then a long silence. My heart sank.

'I don't think this is going to work . . .' he said finally. I couldn't breathe. 'Please don't misunderstand me . . .' he paused. Another deep sigh. 'This is for the best of both of us.'

'How can this be for the best?' I was on the verge of tears. There was a heavy pain, one I couldn't look past. This couldn't be happening. My dream-come-true was falling apart.

'My family will never accept you and you'll never understand them. You should see the girl my brother has married, that's the kind of girl my family would want for me too. You're from a different world . . . my mother has clearly told me so.'

His *mother!*

'What has your mother got to do with any of this? Did you ask your mother's permission before falling in love and proposing to me?' I lashed out at him, tears streaming down my cheeks now, anger and confusion waging a bitter battle in my heart. 'How can you do this to me, to us?'

'I'm sorry, but I've made up my mind,' he said gravely and suddenly I knew it really was over, all of it. 'Please forgive me and try to remain my friend,' he continued. 'I don't want to lose you completely.'

'Then why are you doing this?' I howled into the phone. 'Who says we have to get married? Why are you ruining today, worrying about tomorrow?'

'What do you want me to do? Keep you as my girlfriend until I decide to get married, and then marry somebody else?'

I froze. I had done enough grovelling. Shattered, I told him I never wanted to see his face again, let alone be friends with him. I spent the entire night sprawled on the floor of the dining room, crying. An alarmed Naina called a few friends over to try and cheer me up, but I just lay there like a corpse.

Over the next few weeks I tried every cliché in the book, from drinking myself senseless to working in office round the clock, even dating with a vengeance. None of it worked. I was devastated — an emotion I had simply never known before. The entire saga seemed so grossly unfair to me. Why did my fantasy have to materialise in the first place, only to vanish again? What was the sense in giving it all to me and then snatching it away?

Other little girls grew up dreaming of Prince Charming on a white stallion, for me it had always been a knight in shining Nike attire. He had come and gone. Just like that.

Thirteen

Home Run

I was in mourning, grieving my break-up with Nasir Naqvi, international cricketer, superstar and celebrity. In my attempt to get over him I had written down a list of top ten reasons why I should forget him, and taped the note to my desk; the poor grammar, the orthodox background, etc. The number one reason on that list, however, the one that inspired me most effectively was: He will be an *ex-cricketer* some day.

Unfortunately I also knew that day would be at least another five to ten years in the coming. So either I had to get him back, or get over him. Pronto. On the surface, I was already enjoying the single days again; blazing a trail on the dating scene, furthering my blossoming career, living it up with my housemate Naina and our oddball ensemble of friends. I even had a dog – Naina and I bought a darling golden retriever to lavish attention upon and named him Kaiserslautern after the German football club.

It was liberty like we had never experienced before – we were single working women in the bustling metropolis of New Delhi, with ambition in our hearts, independence in our lives and cash in our wallets. Life was good, but I didn't acknowledge it for what it was. I was still too preoccupied with counting my mistakes with Nasir, trying to pinpoint where it had gone wrong, how I could have let such a catch slip, pardon the pun.

'No ordinary guy is ever going to measure up,' I would tell Naina forlornly.

I was sure of that, and lived in eternal anticipation of the day Nasir would come back to me, grovelling and begging on all fours. Then the entire Indian cricket team would attend our nuptials and we would be the toast of the nation. Sigh. I withered away many a day visualising various versions of this tale.

Nasir and I, incredibly, remained friends despite the break-up, all thanks to him. I didn't know why he made it a point to keep in touch, but I was grateful for it – it allowed me hope to hang on to. On his part, perhaps it was guilt, or maybe he did genuinely miss me too. Either way, he called frequently, irrespective of which corner of the globe he was in, and we kept each other updated on our lives. My profession certainly didn't alleviate my suffering either. Being a sports journalist involved keeping track of the dozen or so worshipped and chastised men on the Indian cricket team. This essentially meant I had Nasir in my face the whole time, while he didn't have to bear such a burden.

Nevertheless, I loved my job. I toiled hard as a rookie reporter, working on junior tennis, domestic cricket and golf. I was overworked and loved every minute of it. And my latest posse of friends also provided quite a distraction; otherwise I might have permanently lost my marbles. I had grown close to Naina and Pranav's set of comrades from Lucknow. Once Naina moved in with me, it seemed that Delhi's entire population had been taken over by people from Lucknow – every person I met from then on seemed to hail from the ancient town of the *nawabs*. It was like a colonisation. Not that I was complaining. This Lucknow bunch really amused me – they were close-knit like a thick woollen sweater, and that despite the fact that all of them had been in love with all the others at some point or the other in their lives. In fact, I used to jest with Naina that hers was the most incestuous flock I'd ever known. Their convoluted amorous pasts notwithstanding, they were all warm, witty and fun.

They were all also aware of my tragic split; I made no attempt whatsoever to conceal my misery.

One rainy Sunday evening, Naina and I chatted dejectedly over cups of tea, Kaiserslautern dozing near our ankles. I wasn't the only one coping with a rotten love life. Naina too, although far less dramatic, was going through a turbulent phase. She had been allowing the same playboy to break her heart again and again for over a year. I begged her to cut him off but my pleas didn't register.

My mobile rang and jolted us out of our daze, Kaiser included. It was Sunil, my colleague. He was the senior cricket writer at *Hindustan*, who had benevolently taken me under his wing. He was also my only colleague who knew about Nasir and me.

'Did you know that your boyfriend is sleeping with that model Honey Khan?' he said in his characteristic dour, insensitive manner. My heart shut down instantly. I knew he had just returned from an international tour where he would have been privy to inside information on the players' extra-curricular activities. But this was hardly what I wanted to hear.

'What do you mean?' I gasped. 'How do you know?'

'The whole bloody city knows. It's in our weekend magazine. Didn't you read it?'

I told him I hadn't and immediately hung up. Naina, Kaiser and I made a mad dash to the living room and grabbed the as yet unread copy of the Sunday Magazine. There it was! On the first page, the scoop of the week. Apparently this tramp Honey had met Nasir during a party in Mumbai before the tour and they had been SMS-ing each other frenziedly ever since. She had even flown to New Zealand for the final of the One-Day series.

'We're just good friends,' was the dumb, obvious quote in the article. But you could almost hear the giggles in the background.

I was too shocked to react. Without a word I ran into the bedroom, pulled on my sneakers and darted past Naina and Kaiser, out the door before either could blink.

Outside, I stood for a moment; face up in the downpour that had started just moments back, soaking it in, each stab of the rain both startling and enlivening. I flipped up the hood of my jacket and then I was off, sprinting in the rainstorm like a madwoman.

I ran past the Chor Minar, a beautiful old ruin tucked away in a nondescript corner of Hauz Khas, onto the August Kranti Marg. The main artery of South Delhi traffic was virtually deserted, only an occasional car gleaming in the flash of lightning. The street lamps had all gone out. Although it was only about seven in the evening, it felt like midnight. Howling winds, crackling thunder, and an insane cloudburst – it was as if the perfect set had been crafted to reflect my mood.

And so I ran, past the Siri Fort auditorium, past Khel Gaon, the former Asian Games Complex where I had first made my acquaintance with sport, more than twenty years ago. Images of that football match flashed before my eyes as I ran faster. Slowly, anger and hurt began to wash away in the rivulets that the rainwater formed from my brow to my toes. A new feeling began to trickle in — calm. Peace. Power. I ran faster, beyond Delhi's first ever mall — the Ansal Plaza — and crossed over the Inner Ring Road. My head cleared as if mould accumulating between my ears for a million years had just been wiped clean.

The imposing enormity of the Jawaharlal Nehru Stadium forced me to a halt, looming large as I came down the flyover connecting Defence Colony and the famed Sai Mandir. I paused for breath and to grasp just how far I had come. And then, in the flash of lightning, I had a thought.

And all alone, drenched to the bone, exhausted, I began to smile.

'I'm going to run the Delhi Marathon!' I exclaimed as soon as Naina opened the door, concern and confusion writ large in her expressive brown eyes. Kaiser was beside her, barking and wagging his tail to welcome my return.

'What marathon?' Naina said, still by the open door even as I rushed in, forming large puddles behind me on the marble floor. 'What are you doing? Where did you go?'

The entire Lucknow brigade — Pranav, Aruna, Kabir, Sasha and Manav — had meanwhile assembled in our living room. Apparently, I had worried Naina more than I had cared to believe. I beamed at all of them.

'I ran!' I announced, smiling. 'I ran like I haven't run in ten years. And it's the best feeling in the world. So I'm going to run the marathon!'

'That's great,' Naina replied, always wary of my excitability, but trying to be supportive and not really sure where this was going.

'When is that?' Pranav inquired, disregarding my sodden condition.

'And how much do you have to run?' Aruna added. 'I mean, what distance?'

'It's in November I think, exactly six months from now. It's perfect! I have enough time to train. And its forty-two kilometres.'

'Forty-two!' The tall, handsome Sasha's eyes nearly popped out of his head.

'Do you have any idea what it takes to be able to run forty-two kilometres?' a sardonic baritone emanated from near the corner of the room.

Manav, I knew it. It could only have been him. He was the only one among Naina's friends who irritated me and got under my skin. He had known Naina and Pranav since their diaper days but was not a very frequent visitor to our pad. Naina said he had kind of drifted away from the troupe a few years ago, and was only now carrying out a homecoming of sorts. It – the fallout – had had something to do with a mistrustful girlfriend who wouldn't let him near any of his female friends. But since that relationship had now gone kaput, he was renewing his friendships with his childhood gang. Not that I gave a hoot.

'I know what it takes,' I said, crossly. 'I used to run ten kilometres' cross country easily at school.'

'School . . .' he said, implying everything and not saying anything.

'I know that was a long time ago, but believe me, I can do this!' I said, hugging my wet knees, suddenly deciding that I was not going to let this surly man ruin my mood. 'And there's also a senior citizen's run of three kilometres which I'm planning to register you for.'

And everyone burst into laughter.

Manav was boyishly cute, but far too reticent, curt and virtuous for my liking. And more importantly, he always ignored me. So most of the time he visited us, I returned the favour and went about doing something far more productive, like sit-ups or squats, or at other times, lying on the floor with Nasir's portrait and whimpering. Like a classic lunatic, my days oscillated wildly between euphoria, when I trained, and total despondency otherwise.

Once, after witnessing my pathetic behaviour on more than one occasion, Manav suggested to Naina in all seriousness, 'Maybe she needs professional help.'

I hit the roof when Naina conveyed his observation. I asked her to tell him to get his own head examined and would have loved to give him a piece of my mind, but apparently he was travelling for some stupid amateur golf tournament and would not be back in town for a couple of weeks or more.

'Huh! Amateur golf!' I scorned. 'Who plays *amateur* sport in their mid-20s?' Clearly, I had not looked in the mirror lately.

Meanwhile, my rebuilding continued. At first I started with trying to run five kilometres in a decent time. It was tougher than I thought. It took me weeks and not days to clock a respectable seventeen minutes. After that, my target was to push the distance by a kilometre every alternate day. I remembered from my school training that there were two basic principles in preparing for a long distance race: gradually increasing your daily running distance and systematically working on achieving a decent weekly mileage total, around 30-35 kilometres per week.

There were other workouts to be followed of course, like stretching and yoga for injury prevention, weight training at least twice a week, and focused eating – pulled straight out of a Sports

Nutrition Guidebook. It was going well, I knew it. And the better I felt about myself, the lesser time I spent wallowing in the depths of despair.

I would often worry about Naina though and what she was letting her man do to her. Their clandestine affair continued, without the slightest emotional investment from his end. In any case, he was cheating on his girlfriend, who was not Naina. I begged her to break it off. Naturally, my pleas fell on deaf ears – love is not *only* blind. It was as if she was caught in a web and didn't know it herself. There were more days than I cared to count when I would wake up and stumble to the kitchen in search of my morning cuppa, only to find Naina sitting by herself at the dining table, crying silently. I wanted to give this chap a jolly good hiding. It almost came to that.

One Friday when Naina wasn't home yet from work, the jerk pushed his luck a little too far by demonstrating the audacity to make a pass at me! Incensed out of my mind, I threw him out, forbidding him from ever setting foot in our house again.

To my utter disbelief and disappointment, when I related the development to Naina later that evening, she turned on me instead.

'How could you do this to him?' she screamed at me. 'How could you do this to me?'

I was obviously missing something here. I thought I had been the Fairy Godmother. By the end of the evening, I found to my further dismay that all my 'Lucknow' mates turned out to be fair-weather friends. Naina marched out of the house to bunk over at someone else's place and the rest of the brood assembled there. Apparently no one was speaking to me for some inexplicable reason, which I discovered upon making a few phone calls, in an effort to muster some company for the evening. I couldn't believe it – these guys were thicker than molasses, a total lack of rationale notwithstanding.

I was left stranded, alone, confused, and depressed. To make matters worse, I discovered that I had lost my cell phone somewhere along the day. My cell phone was my lifeline – my only connect with Nasir. We had resumed our so-called 'friendship' after he had convinced me that the Honey Khan rumours were just that. And I had latched onto a rekindled hope.

'Just wonderful, icing on the cake,' I thought despairingly, stroking Kaiser, who looked up at me with soulful eyes that seemed to say, 'I know how you feel.'

I used the landline to put a call through to my cousin Kartik – heck, I had childhood friends too, who did these people think they were? Kartik opportunely, was in Chandigarh for the weekend. Brilliant. Now what? Lonely didn't begin to describe how I felt. Maybe I should call up a colleague and step out for a stiff drink, I thought. Just then the doorbell rang. Never in my life had I been so glad to hear that mundane sound. There was another human being out there! I practically flew to the door.

'Hi,' said Manav, warily smiling at me, and then searching behind me for other traces of life. 'Where's everyone?' Our house was the established Friday night hangout. Manav, clearly, was oblivious of recent proceedings.

'They're all at Aruna's house,' I tried to sound as unruffled as possible.

'Why?' he was puzzled. 'I mean, then why aren't you there?'

'BECAUSE THEY ALL HATE ME!' I burst into tears with a loud sob and for a moment Manav looked so alarmed I thought he was going to do an about-turn and run for his life. But he only stepped inside and shut the door behind him calmly.

'What's wrong?' There was so much composure in his voice that it only made me wail louder.

'That's absurd,' he stated matter-of-factly after I had recounted the entire episode to him, crouched on a chair at the dining table. 'I can still understand why Naina might be upset, but why is everyone else behaving like that with you?'

'Because they're all joined at the hip since birth,' I bawled at him. 'You should know, you're one of them.'

'No I'm not,' he said sternly. 'They are my friends, but it's this business of huddling together only because we've known each other for twenty years that I find ridiculous.'

'Exactly!' I shouted, jumping off my chair and wiping away my tears. 'Imagine how ludicrous all this seems to me. I moved around all my life so I never had friends last longer than three or four years. But so what? They mean as much to me as you guys probably do to each other. I'm so fond of this bunch. I can't believe they've all turned against me, just like that.'

'To me, it's the quality of their friendship that matters,' Manav continued. 'Not the number of years.'

I couldn't believe my ears. Here was a *bona fide* Lucknow person, who actually saw things with the same perspective as the rest of the human race. Suddenly it dawned upon me that this man standing before me was atypical in more ways than one. For starters, he was studying to be a social worker. Who does that? No one I knew. Then there was that absolute reluctance to make a drunken fool of himself at social gatherings, something other young men our age revelled in doing. Add to that the realisation that he had never attempted to flirt with me, and suddenly I was gazing at this unforthcoming man with newfound respect. He had a mind of his own.

'And I lost my cell phone today too,' I told him, grateful for the sympathy I seemed to be garnering and hoping to cash in on some more. 'And now I won't know if Nasir tries to call me.'

'He still calls you?' Manav questioned, intrigued.

'Of course,' I said indignantly. What did he think? That I was hanging onto imaginary threads of hope. Oh no sir, my relationship was far from over. Nasir just hadn't realised it yet.

'Would you like to go out for a drink?' he asked suddenly.

'Now you're talking.'

Over the next few days, Manav called the house regularly and made polite conversation with me, although I suspected in reality he was checking on me to make sure I hadn't slit my wrist or something to that effect. Happily enough, Naina too returned home a couple of days later and we laughed and made up. We credited the whole mess to the fact that a woman in love can be completely illogical and absurd.

Needless to say, the rest of the party came bouncing along as well. They even presented me with a new phone, while the network provider thankfully restored my old number. I was just so grateful for everything to have returned to normal that I didn't have space in my heart to hold a grudge. But I had acquired a new friend. Manav and me became friends from then on, and I let him in on my pain. To my surprise I discovered that it was entirely possible to be in sorrow and not make a song and dance about it – apparently he was going through the same trough. His girlfriend for five years, Shilpa, had gone off to London to study and had simply disappeared from his life, no formal break-up, no nothing. Like me, Manav too was broken-hearted,

I was whisked along that summer on the annual Lucknow People's Pilgrimage to the hill station of Nainital, and I happily spent much of that holiday training in the hills, running uphill, strengthening my legs and lungs. On rainy days I whiled away time watching the football World Cup in South Korea and Japan, where Brazil won its fifth title, defeating my beloved Germany in the final. The same summer Serena Williams won Wimbledon, the second of three titles she would win that year, asserting her supremacy on women's tennis. And I also watched cricket. There was simply no getting away from it. I missed Nasir terribly but my friends refused to hear another word about him.

Kabir and me were returning to Delhi much before everybody else. The two of us had been granted shorter leaves. Exhausted from our drive home, which had included a terrific 7-hour traffic jam, we stopped over at Manav's because he hadn't come along with the rest of us to Nainital. I was also looking forward to meeting him – at least that was one sympathetic ear. In his characteristic style, Manav met us at the gate, sporting a stubble and pyjamas, playing with his adopted stray dog, Juhi.

After idly watching TV for a while Kabir suggested we get a move-on. I told him I was staying put and watched his jaw drop.

'You're going to stay overnight?' he asked incredulous. 'Here?'

'Yeah,' I replied nonchalantly. I realised it might seem improper, especially if I didn't even seek the homeowner's permission. So I asked Manav. 'It's okay with you, isn't it?'

Manav simply shrugged an okay, but the look in his eyes told me he was a bit baffled. Kabir left soon after, looking at me out of the corner of his eye even as he said bye, wondering what incalculable horror I was planning on inflicting upon his poor friend. I wasn't planning anything. I really just wanted to stay and chat. And as far as it seeming inappropriate was concerned, never in my life had I let such convention bother me and I wasn't about to start then.

We stayed up late and chatted. I told him about the Nainital trip, he filled me in on the recent political developments in the country. I feigned interest. We were having a good time when out of the blue my new cell phone rang and I saw Nasir's number flashing. Never did it fail to make me skip a heartbeat.

'Hello?' I answered the phone and excitedly gestured to Manav that it was Nasir's call — a cue for him to exit the room. He courteously complied.

'Where are you calling from?' I asked Nasir breathlessly. I knew the team was on a tour of Sri Lanka, but I didn't know which city they were in that day.

'Kandy,' he said and I immediately pictured the pretty hill station. I had been there with him last year. 'You know what happened . . .'

And he went onto describe his activities as he usually did, gave me the latest in his ongoing cold war with the coach and made me laugh with impersonations of the Lankan cricketers until my sides ached. Our break-up was a mere formality; in reality things had hardly changed. I was still very much part of his life. We talked for almost half an hour before he hung up saying he had to go to bed as they had an early practice session the next morning.

I called Manav back into the room and just as I was about to unload all the details of my conversation with him, the phone rang again. This time it was his cell phone — an international number. He frowned and picked it up. Upon hearing the voice at the other end, he looked like the wind had got sucked out of his lungs and

I knew instantly that it was his ex-girlfriend, Shilpa. Odd. I wasn't aware that they too were still in touch.

They seemed to be making polite conversation though, as if they hadn't spoken in ages. Manav was mumbling something insignificant and not making much progress in the exchange. She had called him, he had the upper hand – didn't he *see* that? I decided to help him along a bit and knowing fully well that nothing works better than envy, started talking loudly to myself and making lots of noise. Manav was appalled, no clue what on earth I was doing. Irritated, he even put his finger to his lips to try and shut me up.

'Oh, no one,' he said distractedly into the phone. This was it! She had inquired who was with him. Silly boy, didn't he know what he was supposed to do?

'Tell her I'm your girlfriend,' I whispered to him, animatedly. He looked perplexed for a moment, and then apparently caught on.

'That's uh . . . that's my girlfriend,' he said, not very convincingly, and I slapped my forehead in frustration. If he was going to sound so unsure about it, she was certainly not going to fall for it.

'Tell her my name!' I ordered him.

He did. And it worked like magic. Shilpa, instantly jealous, shrieked at him and said, 'I don't call for a few months and you go and get yourself a new girlfriend?'

Manav reminded her that for the past one year he was the one who had made all the effort and that she had categorically told him it was over. Unexpectedly, she said she wanted to speak to me.

To me! What for?

'Hi, this is awkward,' I said to her, trying to sound like a bimbo just for the fun of it. Bimbos irritate women more than any other breed of 'other woman'. 'What do you want to talk about?'

'What the hell do you think I want to talk about?' she snapped at me. Omigosh, this woman was a holy terror. 'Who are you? Are you really his girlfriend or just his cousin or something?'

'Why would he call his cousin his girlfriend,' I asked her, remembering at once that I too, a million years ago had pretended that my cousin Kartik was my boyfriend. Couldn't remember what kind of a situation had demanded such tackiness.

'I don't believe this,' she fumed, clearly shocked out of her skull. 'How long have you been seeing him?'

'Oh, a couple of months . . .' I said, suppressing a giggle. Manav too was smiling lazily.

'Are you going to marry him?' she barked in a tone that implied a threat. As if an answer in the affirmative would be the end of my days. What a lame-O. What was he doing, being in love with her?

'Why don't you ask him?' I retorted and passed the phone back to Manav, having had enough of Attila the Hun. 'She wants to know if we're planning to get married,' I giggled and left the room, to allow him his share of privacy.

My spontaneous plan turned out to be a stroke of genius. Not only did the hysterical woman shift from being furious to incredulous to apologetic to beseeching in the space of fifteen minutes, she told him outright that she was coming back to India shortly in the fall, and was going to stake her claim on what was rightfully hers. Manav looked exceptionally happy and I was thrilled with myself.

What a darling little Cupid I was. Then I decided if it could work for him, it could work for me too. Of course! Manav and I spent much of the night discussing strategies, and the plans were laid. Pleased as punch, I went to bed dreaming of a rosy future where I would be reunited with my lost love.

In the morning as I met Manav in his garden, a new fear crept over me. There was a possibility I hadn't even considered.

'Don't fall for me,' I told him with sudden brusqueness. 'You know, like in that movie *French Kiss?*'

'What are you talking about?' he was still groggily rubbing his eyes. 'I haven't seen whatever movie that is.'

'There is this Meg Ryan movie where two friends decide to help each other, exactly the way we have planned,' I told him. 'But they end up falling for each other. Please don't fall for me, okay? This is not a movie.'

'*You* better not fall for me,' he replied gravely, as if that were a more likely possibility. Excuse me. Did he know who he was speaking to? Fat chance. Although I was relieved he felt the same way, I didn't get much of an opportunity to dwell on the subject because out of nowhere he hurled a football at me and we plunged into an impromptu one-on-one match.

Our extraordinary plan worked like magic both ways. Nasir responded favourably too, although not as rabidly as Shilpa. He was in London, where the team was just embarking on a Test tour, and I too, was supposed to be holidaying there with my parents in couple of weeks' time. All I had to do was set the stage before I made my grand re-entrance into his life. It was time to break the 'news'.

'By the way, I have two interesting things to tell you,' I said after we had exchanged the initial pleasantries. 'First, I am running the Delhi International Marathon.'

Nasir laughed at the other end,.

'What is so funny?' I demanded. 'I have been training like mad and I'm in good shape. I may even do very well, you know.'

'Okay, very good,' he said, still laughing. 'Maybe you'll win and become a bigger star than me.'

Huh? I knew that the stardom, the money and all the attention had been slowly getting to his head. I had noticed it gradually even while we had been seeing each other, but had chosen to ignore it. However, he had never said anything condescending to me until then.

'Why do you think everything is about you?' I was infuriated. 'I have no interest in attaining some exalted celebrity status; I like my normal life very much, thank you. Anyway, no one even cares who wins a marathon. I want to run because it makes me happy. Get it?'

He grunted something inarticulate, as he always did when at a loss for words. I wanted to get on with the conversation, drop the bomb.

'And the other thing,' I said. 'You remember my friend Manav whom I had told you about?'

'Yes, the golfer. What about him?'

'He's not a golfer, he's social worker. Anyway, he asked me out and . . . I said yes,' I held my breath for a reaction. None came. 'I'm going out with him.'

After a long pause Nasir quietly said, 'What do you mean? Is he your boyfriend?'

'Yes,' I replied succinctly, waiting to gauge his sentiment.

'I'm happy for you,' Nasir said after another long pause, but the disappointment and surprise in his voice were unmistakable. Ha. I had him right where I wanted.

'Will you still meet me when you come to London?' he asked tentatively.

'Of course,' I replied smugly. 'We're still friends, right?'

I had actually quit my job to be able to go for this two-month long family vacation in the UK and United States. And I wasn't worried because a new position as assistant sports producer waited for me at a television news station when I got back. When my parents had planned their trip, I knew I simply had to go along, to get a chance to be with Nasir again.

When we finally did meet, and this was after a gap of almost a year, it was as if nothing had changed, time had stood still. We went out for dinners and dancing, talked and joked and strolled down Knightsbridge till two in the morning. Only, I was doing all this with him as 'someone else's girl' and Nasir was only too aware of that. He didn't make a move nor said anything. I was bitterly disappointed.

After a week or so in London, my parents and I were off to the US to visit my sister Shiny and cousin Saurav, who were now living and studying in New York and Los Angeles respectively. I made a resolution to not call Nasir the entire time I was in America and miraculously, I found the pluck to stick to the decision. Let him squirm. I did call Manav several times though, who profusely congratulated me on my London exploits.

Come September and I was back home in Delhi, eager to get back to my training regime. It was now just over a month to go for the marathon and I had to up my weekly mileage from forty-five kilometres to sixty. Through my entire trip I had continued to run whenever possible, clocking fifteen kilometres every alternate day, punctuated with rest days in between. It was all coming together, I could feel it in my bones.

I also had to fill Manav in on all that had come about in the last two months, both Nasir and non-Nasir related information. I called him as soon as I touched down in Delhi to inform him that I would be coming over that evening. But he said I couldn't, not that evening, because guess who was dropping by?

'She's here?' I screeched into my phone. 'Shilpa's already here? When did she arrive?'

'Just yesterday,' he said. He sounded in such good cheer. 'In fact, she should be here any minute now.'

'Well then I can visit you in the evening, can't I?' I said shakily. 'I mean, it's just ten in the morning right now.'

'I haven't seen her in a year,' Manav spoke patiently, as though explaining a difficult concept to a dim-witted child. 'I think we might spend the whole day together.'

Why my heart sank at that statement I didn't know. But it did all right. I reprimanded myself – it was only natural he would want to spend at least one whole day patching up a relationship that had meant so much to him. How selfish of me not to have understood that immediately.

'Oh, all right then,' I said trying to sound far more cheerful than I felt. 'I guess I'll see you tomorrow or day after. All the best. I know it's going to work out for you two.'

'Thanks a lot,' he said. 'For everything.'

By afternoon I couldn't bear it any longer. I had to call him, just to know how things had progressed.

'Hi, can you talk?'

'Umm, yeah for a minute,' Manav replied, sounding preoccupied.

'Oh? Shilpa's still there?' I asked. Obviously she was. 'I just wanted to know if everything turned out fine.'

'Yeah it did, it has,' I could tell he was smiling now. 'It's great. We've made up, we're back together. I still can't believe it. . . . It's all thanks to you.'

'Oh don't be silly. That's fantastic!' I said. 'Congratulations. But what about me? I mean, she must have asked about me.'

'And I've told her the truth,' he said. 'I told her everything was just a lie to get her back.'

And then he hung up. I had to bite my lip to stop myself from crying. Why was I feeling so awful? I couldn't understand it. I was genuinely happy for him, I really was, so why was I so unhappy? I realised I was jealous. Not of her, but of them. The fact that they were officially back together. When would my happy ending with Nasir come? It had better happen soon or I would go stark raving mad, I was sure of that.

I went out with the Lucknow mob that night, to our favourite watering hole Mezz. And amidst the din of the live rock music, I kept bugging Pranav to call Manav and find out whether or not Shilpa was still with him. Pranav simply refused to do something so inane.

'Let them be,' he admonished me. 'Why are you behaving like this?'

As I got more inebriated and more despondent, I couldn't for the life of me, figure out why I felt so forlorn.

Mornings always brought with them good cheer and I woke at six every alternate day to put on my running shoes and run like the wind for an hour or so. I knew the day was coming closer when I would have to attempt the entire distance. It would have to be done at least twice before the actual race, in the two weeks preceding it. Any more and I would deplete my reserves too much. I had already lost close to five kilos.

Forty-two kilometres was a gruelling, demanding distance. Once you ran it, you needed three to four days of rest just to recover.

So I would have to plan the last three weeks very carefully. My friends had formed a certified cheerleading squad by now and not one of them doubted that I could do it. They egged me on, helped in any way they could and a couple of them even signed up for the seven-kilometre Great Delhi Run. Manav was nowhere in the picture though, as I met him less and less. I assumed he was preoccupied with the renaissance of his love affair. I too, was engrossed with mine for that matter. Nasir's phone calls were becoming increasingly frequent again – he had been miffed that I had not kept in touch while holidaying in the States. The team was in the West Indies now and it was more difficult to stay connected, what with the 12-hour time difference, but he still made a point to call often, either early in the morning before my run, or late at night. So things were certainly looking up.

And I was keeping myself absorbed with work too. The new job was promising – not only had I been drafted in at double my previous salary, but they were also training me to become a sports news presenter, a bonus that was entirely unexpected and totally welcome. I toiled long and hard, working twelve-hour days.

On a mid-October afternoon, my executive producer, Udayan called me into his office.

'We want you to cover the Delhi Marathon live,' he stated absently, while rummaging about in his desk for something. Then, pulling out a copy of the press release from the sponsors, he said, 'We'll want you to move in the OB van and follow as much of the course as is possible. It starts at India Gate.... '

'I know the route,' I butted in. 'I'm running it.'

'Running what? The marathon?'

Okay here it comes, I thought – another sceptical man, doubting my ability, ready to leap into ridicule.

'That's fantastic!' He jumped up and thumped his desk, his usually deadpan features breaking into a delightful smile. I was totally taken aback. 'The full marathon?' he asked.

'Yes,' I said, a bit unsure of how to handle this sudden buoyancy. 'I've been training; I'm definitely going to finish it.'

'Can you win it?' he asked, completely startling me.

'Win it?' I asked back, blinking at him. Was he serious?

'Yes, you do run a race to win it, don't you?'

No you don't, I wanted to tell him, not a marathon. You run a marathon to finish it. But there was no point in trying to explain that to this archetypal, competitive Indian male whose only comprehension of sport was cricket.

So I said, 'I think that's the sole birthright of the Kenyans,' and we both laughed. At least he got that one.

'All right Tanya Trivedi, very funny,' he smirked, sitting back down. 'There is a separate category for Indian runners, you know? And a sub-category within that, for women. Can you win that?'

Now this was something I really didn't know. Maybe he knew more than I gave him credit for. Or then again, it was all probably written there in that press release.

'I think I can,' I answered his question in all seriousness. 'I don't know the national times but I have been training with the standard international times in mind. I really think, maybe I can.'

'Well that's bloody fantastic then,' he said, excited as though there was a serious possibility of him winning it himself, portly frame and all. 'We'll build our whole coverage around you, get another reporter to track you all the way, you can wear our channel logo on your shirt, and maybe we can even strap a wireless mike onto you . . .'

Almost dizzy from this sudden development, I started to retreat out of his office, while he continued ranting. Just as I was about to step out into the common production area, I tripped over the door ledge.

Snap.

A white hot bolt of pain.

I fell to the floor with a thud, screaming in pain. Within seconds several colleagues had encircled me and were trying to lift me back up. Udayan came running out of his office. I yelped as I attempted to stand up, grabbing hold of my right ankle which had twisted under my own weight. I was in excruciating agony and I looked down to check the damage. It was already swollen and suddenly I was in tears.

'Oh no, Tanya Trivedi!' Udayan said, almost mocking. 'I hope you didn't do this on purpose.'

Hobbling, I glared up at him.

I wanted to slap him.

It was a nasty sprain all right, but the good news was that nothing had broken. A fracture would have been the cruellest joke the universe could have played on me. This was bad enough. As I sat in bed at home, my ankle heavily strapped, Naina and the gang rallied around me with cups of tea and cheerful optimism.

'Don't worry, you'll be back on your feet in three weeks,' Naina said. 'Didn't the doctor say so?'

'I don't have three weeks!' I snapped at her, again on the verge of tears at my predicament. 'The race is in three weeks! If all I do for the next three weeks is sit in bed, there is absolutely no way I'm going to be able to run it!'

The phone rang and interrupted my whimpering. It was Manav. I hadn't heard from him in weeks and lashed out.

'Where the hell have you been? Just because your girlfriend is back in your life doesn't mean you forget all your friends!'

'I heard you hurt yourself,' he said calmly, concerned.

'Hurt is an understatement,' I wailed. 'I don't know which idiot told you that. I haven't just hurt myself; I've finished my chances of running the marathon.'

'How long did the doctor say before you can walk?' he asked. Walking? How would that help? Nevertheless, I answered.

'Well, he said I can move about in a week, but he's really not sure if I can run even in three.'

'If you can move about in a week, you will run in three,' he said and hung up without another word or further explanation.

Two hours later Manav was at our pad, tempo in tow, unloading some monstrosity packed in cardboard and bubble sheets into my living room. Kaiser ran around it in circles, very suspicious. Manav pulled the wrapping off and it was a stationary bike! In spite of my foot I jumped up and hugged him. No one else understood the implication but I did.

'Don't you see?' I turned to everyone in delight. 'I can continue training, stay in shape, without putting pressure on my foot!'

Comprehension dawned on a couple of fellows.

'But it's not the same as running,' Sasha said circumspectly.

'Of course it's not!' I replied. 'But it's the next best thing. Swimming and stationary cycling is what even professional athletes do for rehab – to recover from injury and stay conditioned. If anything, it will make my legs stronger.'

'Oh thank you, Manav!' I bear-hugged him again and we both looked fondly into each other's eyes for a few moments. I felt something stir in my heart. I had missed him so much. He had better start hanging out again, even if it meant bringing that Shilpa along. He was just such a darling, responsible person to have around.

'You should be on that thing for two hours a day at least,' he said roughly, but he was smiling, his arms still around mine. 'You've been training like a psycho for six months, we're not going to let two weeks change that.'

'You bet!' I said happily and clapped my hands in delight.

November in the capital is beautiful, like a song. The air feels cold and clean, the wide avenues of Central Delhi are carpeted with gold-and-rust leaves, and the sky takes on a handsome grey-blue hue.

It was on precisely such an idyllic morning that thousands of people assembled at the start line of the Delhi International Marathon – the point where the majestic Rajpath intersects the hexagon of India Gate. D-day had dawned upon me before I felt entirely ready. Hundreds of professional runners from around the world had flown in. The Kenyans were in full force, their green, red and white kits distinguishing them from the rest of the crowd. Europeans, Asians and hundreds of our very own. Banners and posters fluttered about everywhere. An air balloon floated past the clouds telling all and sundry to 'Feel the Spirit'. Sponsors' trucks and TV crew vans jostled for space. Colours everywhere; people, old and young. It was like a gigantic carnival.

I stood at my spot, shaking my arms and legs to rid them of the nerves that were threatening to cramp me up. My right ankle was still heavily strapped but I had been able to run ten kilometres the day before without pain. I was as geared up as I was going to get. Pranav and Sasha thumped me on the back and wished me luck — they too were getting ready for the Great Delhi Run a little later in the morning.

My good friend and colleague from the sports desk, Chandru, was there, mike in hand, shadowed by the cameraman. He talked into the camera and introduced me; I was live on my channel.

'So, Tanya,' he said, turning to me. 'Can you predict a time for yourself?'

'Oh no!' I laughed, theatrical for the benefit of the camera. 'I'm not going to make any predictions. I just want to finish the race and not be the last one to do so.'

A hoisted flag signalled the start of the marathon and the atmosphere exploded into a collective roar of thousands. I plugged in my earphones and set off. It was important to sprint at the start, to break away from the masses before getting trapped. I accelerated at a speed that I would not be able to maintain for more than five to ten minutes and was instantly alarmed as I felt a twinge of protest from my dubious ankle. This is not good, I thought to myself, running hard to keep up with those who like me, were trying to get ahead of the pack at the very start. But the pain was momentary and it passed as soon as I settled into the rhythm of Eye of the Tiger — my favourite tunes of all time were systematically stacked in the iPOD strapped onto my arm, planned to build up to a crescendo at the hundred and twenty minute mark.

We ran along half the India Gate circle — a collective river of colour, channelled by the bright orange cones that formed the route, contained by the yellow ropes strung along the sidewalks and intersections.

'Go India, go!' came a collective chant from behind the ropes, encouraging us indigenous runners to fare well.

We went around the Dhyan Chand National Stadium, and then right onto Mathura road. The route was dead straight after this point for the next ten kilometres. My feet moved automatically to the beat imposed by the song that thumped in my head.

Half an hour later, the serious runners had cleanly disengaged themselves from the also-rans. We had passed Sundernagar and Nizamuddin East and just as we were nearing the congested, industrial belt of Okhla, the route decided to save us the nuisance by turning right onto the Outer Ring Road. Almost a sixth of the initial runners had already dropped out and many more were wilting – there was no way they were going to finish. A few metres ahead of us I saw another colleague of mine, standing behind the ropes at the Nehru Place bus terminal, leaning forward and waving to grab my attention, but all I could hear was 'I'm Blue Da-Ba-Dee-Da-Ba-Da. . . .'

I pulled out one earplug, just in time to hear her yell, 'Tanya, your group is more than a kilometre ahead of the majority of the pack, how does it feel?'

This had to be a joke. Was I really expected to answer that question into the mike she was thrusting at me? It was my channel after all, so I gave a thumbs-up sign and pointed to the channel logo on my vest, all for the benefit of Udayan who was surely watching from the comfort of his home and smirking. He better double my salary after this, I thought. I grabbed one of the bottled mineral drinks that were available for the runners at various points along the route and carried on.

We continued on the Outer Ring Road, past the commercial district of Nehru Place and Ho Chi Minh Marg, right up till the Chirag Delhi flyover. The wide, tree-lined Press Enclave Marg took us past the Lado Sarai Golf Club – the only place in the city which gave cheap access to golf for everyone – and from there we turned right onto Aurobindo Marg.

The halfway mark! This was a huge psychological landmark for those of us in the leader group that were tiring. It already felt like an eternity since we had started running, but the knowledge that we were halfway home bolstered our confidence and reserves. Two Kenyan women, some more African runners and a smattering of Caucasians had sped away from the main leader-group and were already making their way back. Just as I was turning right from under the IIT Flyover, I caught a glimpse of a paunchy, thirty-something man waving and grinning wildly from the sidelines as though he was personally involved with the run. Wait a minute. He was waving directly at me! There was a beautiful woman by his side, elegant even in her pyjamas, who also seemed to be looking straight at me and smiling. She looked so familiar. Was it . . .

'Saira?' I whispered to myself. Could this be the girl whose boyfriend I had stolen back in high school? Hold on a second, the man was 'Sam!' I waved.

Sam and Saira waved again at me, yelling 'Go Tanya!' as I passed them, dumbstruck. I had heard vague stories from old school-friends that Sam had eventually begged Saira's forgiveness and they had married each other a year or two ago. Wow! God bless Saira, I thought, trying to evade a rush of guilt – she has it in her heart to be able to smile at me and cheer me on. Not such a bimbo after all.

From the tip of South Delhi we were making our way back now, mapping a slightly different route. I was beginning to seriously tire, I couldn't deny it. But it wasn't acute enough to alarm me just yet. My feet were running on autopilot now, to the rhythm of 'I Like to Move It, Move It'. Looming large ahead of me, at the gate to the Asian Games Village, was a massive billboard for one of the soft-drink manufacturers that were co-sponsoring the marathon. It featured six members of the Indian cricket team and there, standing right in the middle of the gang was Nasir Naqvi, grinning, airbrushed and 32-feet-tall.

'All right mister,' I said directly to the hoarding. 'I'm going to finish this race, let's see you laugh now.'

Nasir didn't have anything particularly intelligent to say.

Revitalised, I accelerated and immediately left behind a neat group of twelve or thirteen runners. Another five or six promptly caught up with me in a few strides. That was fine; all I wanted was to get the leading women back in my line of vision.

We went straight down the Khel Gaon Marg, our feet numb by now, backs aching and the nine o'clock sun beating down upon us. Another one of my colleagues popped up like a Jack-In-The-Box – Raghu. Raghu was our Entertainment Reporter, and bizarrely enough, the brother of a certain Amit Mehra I had dated for four years. What was this? Judgement Day? Why were the main players from my amorous past appearing all at once?

'Go Tanya! Just another ten kilometres to go!' he yelled, turning around to face his cameraman at the same time, the Nehru Stadium providing a backdrop. I tried to smile at him, but my features had frozen, just like the rest of my body.

What had he said? Was it really just another ten to go? I had the route memorised and had figured where I should be at the two-hour mark. But was I there already? I glanced at the stopwatch on my wrist. 119:32:04. Bang on cue, The Final Countdown came on, marking the start of the home stretch. I was a kilometre or two further down than I had expected to be. This was great news. Considering my lungs were on fire, it really would be nice to finish sometime soon.

The cheers got louder as we moved onto Prithviraj Road and into Central Delhi. Thousands upon thousands of people lined the streets now, elbowing each other out of the way to catch a glimpse of the leaders. One man was messily gobbling a colossal burger right on the ropes and I nearly vomited. Got to keep the blinkers on, I reminded myself and looked straight ahead, trying to shut the world out.

'The men's winner is already home!' a familiar voice shouted out from the crowd, and I turned to find Naina, Kabir and Aruna grinning away at the intersection that led to Khan Market. 'Keep going, you're doing very well!'

It was such a pleasant surprise to see them there, egging me on. It gave me the adrenaline shot I needed and spurred me on faster. I knew I was doing well, there was no doubt about it – only about twenty female runners would finish ahead. But there was still another five kilometres to go and my legs were giving out. My throat was parched and my head felt like lead. This was why it was so important to run the entire distance at least twice before the actual race – you figure your weak moments and how to tackle them. But my darn injury had resulted in me competing without ever having run the entire forty-two. The only consolation was that the ankle had not said a word since its initial whimper in the first five minutes.

I could finally see India Gate! It was the same feeling one got when running a cross-country race that finished inside an athletics track – you knew you had just one more lap to go, before you could allow yourself to collapse in an exhausted heap. The crowd around me was going berserk – clapping, yelling, and waving. The din was deafening, despite my iPOD, which was now onto 2-Unlimited's 'No Limit'. People were leaning over the ropes almost to toppling over. Mad scenes. The finish line was in sight now, with a smattering of athletes who had already finished, strolling about, talking to television reporters, cooling off. At two hours, forty seven minutes and fifty-two seconds I crossed over. Exhaustion, relief and unbridled joy swirled about together in my head. It was over and I had done it! A jubilant throng descended upon me, completely swamping me. I had to gasp for a breath of air. Suddenly there were half a dozen mikes thrust in my face. I felt dizzy.

'. . . Congratulations!'

'. . . How does it feel?'

'. . . Will you represent India in other marathons now?'

'. . . Who is your coach?'

I could not comprehend what was happening. What was going on? Could I get a drink of water? Miraculously, someone handed me a bottle of liquid, as if reading my thoughts. And then Manav materialised out of nowhere. I was so glad to see him; I just collapsed on him, oblivious of all the cameras. He hugged me firmly and then held me at an arm's distance, smiling from ear to ear.

'You won!' he yelled over the cacophony.

'What? No I didn't!' I said, barely able to get the words out.

'You did! You won the Indian women's category!'

'Are you serious?' I said, my heart about to explode. This was unbelievable. 'No way!' I started screaming.

'Excuse me, ma'am, can we have a word with you?' The reporters were back in my face. I howled with delight as I spotted my colleague Chandru and hugged him.

'Headline News first please,' I said merrily, gesturing towards the logo on my chest, and started a live interview with Chandru.

'So you're definitely not the last man and very much the first Indian woman. . . .'

That night, we celebrated wildly, on a high from the improbable developments of the day. By the afternoon I had been on a couple of news channels other than my own and my phone hadn't stopped ringing for even a second. Friends and acquaintances I hadn't spoken to in years tracked me down. Everyone was so happy for me. With the 10,000 US dollars I had pocketed, I wasn't too miserable either. My parents must have called me seven or eight times from Mumbai and the entire Trivedi clan made sure I got no rest in the afternoon either. At 7 p.m. I did a studio show at the Headline News station, Udayan grinning at me all the while from the PCR.

After some heavy partying at Ricks' at the Taj Mansingh, the Lucknow brigade and me retired to the house, where of course, the celebrations continued. Pranav and Sasha had also successfully completed the Great Delhi Run, and a euphoric feeling of accomplishment was in the air.

At about two in the morning my cell phone rang. I ran out into the large terrace balcony, a bitingly cold wind slapping my cheeks.

'Hi ssssweetie,' a distant voice slurred. 'You will be really happy. . .'

'Nasir!' I exclaimed, wondering why he sounded so strange. 'So you've heard?' I was incredulous. How did he get to know all the way in the West Indies?

'Heard what?' he said, still sounding extremely odd.

'I won the marathon!' I danced and skipped as I told him. 'I won the Indian women's category! Can you believe that?'

'Oh that's great,' he said, sounding bored and disconnected.

I felt let down and went very quiet. What was wrong with him? What was wrong with *me*? Why was I still looking for approval from this man who had done nothing but hurt me? Every single turn our relationship had ever taken had been directed by him. All I had done was make that one call that started it all. Then *he* had told me he loved me, *he* had proposed marriage and then *he* had broken up without any explanation.

And even then, he had continued to keep in touch, calling in the middle of the night and other odd hours and all I ever did was wait for the next call. I had absolutely no control whatsoever. And it pained me to realise that I was still holding out for his affection and acceptance.

'Forget it, it doesn't matter,' was all I could say, fighting back tears.

'Tell me, are you happpppy?' he said, as if on some other planet.

'About what?' I snapped. There was something really odd about his voice.

'Are you happy?'

'Nasir, are you drunk?'

'A little bit. . . . '

'What's wrong with you? It's like two in the afternoon for you. Why the hell are you drunk in the middle of the day? What are you doing?'

'Tanya, let's give us another try.'

I had to close my eyes to let it sink in. He didn't know about the marathon. He had called to say he wanted me back. He had said the words I wanted to hear for so long. It had taken more than one year for it to happen, but when it finally had, there was no feeling but vindication. Warm tears ran down my cold cheeks, and the world spun around me.

'Tanya?'

'I'm here.'

'Can we try again?'

'I don't know, Nasir. Maybe. But we'll talk tomorrow when you're sober.'

I trudged back to my friends, lost in a trance. It was all over. The emotional upheaval, the games, the tears and the false bravado, all of it. More than any other emotion, I felt an overwhelming exhaustion. And an inexplicable sadness. As if this wasn't quite the script I had planned. Why?

'Nasir wants me back,' I informed the expectant crowd silently waiting for me in my living room, looking directly at a very dazed Manav.

'That's great news,' he managed to say, half in slumber. 'I'm really, really happy for you.'

Then there was an uncomfortable silence as nobody else said anything.

'Can I talk to you alone?' I asked Manav, and he promptly got up to step out with me.

'Will you miss me?' I asked him, once we were alone.

He didn't respond with something mindless like 'Why? Are you moving?' or 'We'll still be friends.' The few words he said spoke volumes: 'You can only be happy with him.'

Something caught in my throat and I wanted to weep. I asked him to leave me alone and once he did, I did just that – I howled and howled uncontrollably for fifteen minutes out on that dreary cold balcony. Then Naina came out looking for me and found me huddled in a corner, shaking.

'What am I doing?' I wailed. 'Here I am, saying goodbye to the nicest man in the world, for the sake of someone who broke my heart and walked away. Why? Why? Why am I feeling so miserable when everything that I have prayed for in the last one year has just come true?'

Naina, who in any case made her fondness for Manav very apparent, couldn't hide her obvious delight. And it was she who finally made me see the light.

'Call him back out, you fool! And tell him what I already know!'

Suddenly a weight lifted off me. I felt absolute liberation at the mere thought of telling Manav that it was him I didn't want to let go, him I wanted to be with. I immediately darted back indoors and stood square in front of him on the sofa. Who cared if everyone was watching, this was a life-altering moment.

'I want to be with you,' I spoke slowly, looking into his eyes, oblivious of the speechless audience watching the melodrama. 'Not Nasir, you.'

'Tanya, what happened?' Manav stood up, confounded.

'Nothing happened,' I laughed. I wanted to dance. Everybody else was already smiling and chuckling. I continued, 'I just realised that I don't want this to end, this thing that I have with you. I'm sorry if this is the most selfish thing I've ever done. I don't care how happy you are with that Shilpa of yours; I have to tell you that I'm in love with you. And now it's up to you.'

And that is when the gallant gentleman decided to enlighten me that he had never gotten back with Shilpa in the first place. True, they had spent that one day together, trying to piece back what was left of their relationship, but apparently, by the end of the evening he too had succumbed to emotions he hadn't been aware of.

'I'm in love with you too,' Manav said quietly and my heart leapt with joy. Our friends clapped and laughed and hugged both of us, one by one, then hugged each other. Kaiser danced and barked like a mad dog. Everyone was going bananas.

'I told Shilpa that it's over for good that same day, and I've not met her again after that. Not even once.'

I couldn't believe it – the selflessness, and yet, the audacity to lie to me all the while. I wanted to hug and slap him at the same time and for the second time that night, I broke down and wept. Only this time, I was the happiest person in the world. I knew right then and there that I wanted to marry this man. Immediately. Spending the rest of my life with him was going to be such fun, and more importantly, so uncomplicated. Here was a man who had seen me at my absolute worst and had not reported me to an asylum. What more could I ask? I went right down on bended knee and proposed.

'Marry me!'

Manav scooped me up and laughed, 'You are hilarious, don't ever change. And of course, yes, I will marry you.'

Who says fairytales don't come true. Just not the ones you plan in advance.